Ruthless Hearts

Willie Slaughter

Lock Down Publications and Ca$h Presents

Ruthless Hearts

A Novel by *Willie Slaughter*

Willie Slaughter

Lock Down Publications
P.O. Box 870494
Mesquite, Tx 75187

Visit our website @
www.lockdownpublications.com

Lock Down Publications
Like our page on Facebook: Lock Down Publications @
www.facebook.com/lockdownpublications.ldp
Cover design and layout by: **Dynasty Cover Me**
Book interior design by: **Shawn Walker**
Edited by: **Cassandra Sims**

Stay Connected with Us!

Text **LOCKDOWN** to 22828 to stay up-to-date with new releases, sneak peaks, contests and more…

Thank you.

Submission Guideline.

Submit the first three chapters of your completed manuscript to ldpsubmissions@gmail.com, subject line: Your book's title. The manuscript must be in a .doc file and sent as an attachment. Document should be in Times New Roman, double spaced and in size 12 font. Also, provide your synopsis and full contact information. If sending multiple submissions, they must each be in a separate email.

Have a story but no way to send it electronically? You can still submit to LDP/Ca$h Presents. Send in the first three chapters, written or typed, of your completed manuscript to:

LDP: Submissions Dept
Po Box 870494
Mesquite, Tx 75187

DO NOT send original manuscript. Must be a duplicate.

Provide your synopsis and a cover letter containing your full contact information.

Thanks for considering LDP and Ca$h Presents.

DEDICATION

To all my true friends and family. To my ride or die Black Queen, my wife Machumu Harris, I love you, baby girl.

Willie Slaughter

PROLOGUE

At 19 years old, Tabitha Greene stood before her Uncle James with her guard up. Her lip was bloodied, and her left eye had been blackened during the training, but she wasn't giving up. Giving up wasn't in her DNA. At five foot eight, 159 pounds, a cocoa butter complexion and short length hair, she was properly proportioned, some would say walking dynamite.

"Alright Tab, remember, your best defense is your greatest offense. Give me all you got. Don't hold back, because I'm not," James said as he took an offensive stance.

Tabitha put up her guard. "Let's get to it Uncle James."

They circled around one another until, finally, she launched an attack. She threw two quick left jabs and followed up with a spinning heel kick that landed in James' abdominal area. He stumbled backwards. Before he could regain footing, she caught him with a side kick to the chest before jumping on him, taking him down to the ground with a hip toss.

Tabitha backed off from her attack and stood with her hands on her hips smiling. "How you like that Uncle James?"

He got up and dusted himself off. "Tab, you got what it takes to do what you want to do physically. But, don't forget, the heart and mind are two different departments, youngster."

Willie Slaughter

CHAPTER ONE

Tabitha and her Uncle James were done training for the day. They stood out on the front lawn talking for a while until Tabitha's alarm went off on her watch, signaling it was time for her to get to work.

"I'll see you tomorrow morning, Uncle James," she said after hugging him.

"Seven o'clock sharp thunder cat," he replied sarcastically.

She jumped in her Audi 8. When she pushed the ignition button, Icon blared through the Bose car system. She started bobbing her head, hyped off the lyrics and music. James looked on in laughter while watching her back out of the driveway and into traffic.

As he turned to walk up the front porch steps, his cellphone vibrated on his hip. He pulled it out of the case and saw a new text message flash across the screen. He pressed his thumb against the screen to gain access to the inbox. After reading the text, he sighed and pressed the phone receiver icon. The line rang twice before someone answered.

"James, what's going on, my man? How's the family?" the man on the other end of the line said with enthusiasm.

"It's going, Mickey. Everyone's doing fine as far as I know. Let's skip the formalities. What's the problem?" James asked.

Mickey sighed. "Well, it seems that old problems die hard or not at all. You remember that little run-in we had back in Jersey?"

How could he forget? The memory flooded his mind as if it had just happened yesterday...

There he was, 23, six foot even, light skin with freckles, and in the best shape of his life. He and his service partner Mickey Freeman, a 26-year-old, five foot nine, boot-black, and chiseled like a little GI Joe action figure doll, was at the casino in Jersey having a ball.

It had been Mickey's birthday, and every birthday since becoming partners, they would hit the casino wherever the birthday boy decided. That particular birthday, James hadn't paid attention to how much Mickey had drank, however, he knew he wasn't the kind of guy who could handle his alcohol. They had been standing at the blackjack table when two nicely shaped women approached them, smiling seductively. He had brushed off the one pushing up on him, but Mickey was feeling himself so much he palmed the nice round booty of the lady who'd been talking to him, and that's when all hell broke loose.

Turns out, they were two high dollar call-girls working for a well-known guerilla pimp by the name of Silver Fox. Once the girl asked to be compensated for her conversation in addition to him groping her, Mickey ended up pouring his drink on her head before James could intervene. Then, he commenced to yell disrespectful words at her. They hadn't paid attention to the other woman's absence until she returned with two musclebound bodyguards.

James thought he had the situation under control until his partner felt like one of the men had tried to chump him. Something he never took very well, he took flight. James, being the friend he was, jumped in the fight. Finally, the casino's security guards broke up the fight and kicked them out. They ended up finishing the brawl in the parking lot.

"Hello? You still there, James?" Mickey asked, causing James to snap out of his reminiscence of the reckless night. "Yeah, I'm still on the line, bro." He walked on up the stairs and entered the house. "So, what's the issue? Did you go back and finish what you started with that sweet piece of ass you grabbed?"

Mickey laughed. "Man, if I could, I would. But this time I'd be sober. The problem is, the pimp she worked for was found on ice in a meat locker."

James paused in midstride. "Okay. What does that have to do with you or us?"

"More than I care to say over the phone. To be roundabout about the situation, I was hired as a private eye to snoop around and see what I could find out. It was nonnegotiable," Mickey said sounding nervous.

James plopped down on the couch. "What the hell, Mickey? Why would you take such a job knowing damn well the stakes?"

"It was either take the gig, or they were coming for my old lady and my junior. What was I supposed to do?" He replied.

James leaned back on the couch ready for a hot shower and a stiff drink. The answer he wanted to give his old partner wouldn't have been a real solution, but instead, it would've added more fuel to the fire and cause the situation to burn out of control. "Mickey, where are you?"

"You know exactly where I am, Jersey. Actually, about twenty minutes out from Jersey City. I could really use your help on this one J," Mickey said.

With his free hand, James rubbed the back of his neck. It was a sure sign of conflict between the decision he knew he was going to make versus what he really wanted to do. "Sit tight," he told his long-time friend.

He hung up the phone before tossing it on the couch beside him. James knew Mickey too well. There was more to the story than he was telling. Looking at the picture of him and his niece on his screensaver, reminded him of their morning training session. Before he knew it, he had the iPhone X up to his ear.

The "Worst Behavior" ringtone played halfway through before she picked up.

"What's up, Uncle James?" Tabitha said into her phone.

"I gotta take a raincheck on our sessions for a little while. Something came up and I gotta be out of town for a minute. Sorry, Tab," James said.

"No pressure, Uncle James. Keeping it real, I just got a call from the job and I gotta be in Jersey by tomorrow afternoon. Something about a string of meat locker murders," Tabitha replied.

It was either fate, destiny, or something major was happening in the underground world of New Jersey. James juggled the three possibilities in his mind. Finally, he said,

"Looks like we're headed in the same direction. Any chance of you swinging by and us riding together?"

"That's a bet. What time is it?" she asked.

James checked the time. "2:27 pm."

"Give me an hour and forty-five minutes," she told him.

"Waiting on you, youngster," he replied before hanging up.

He tossed the phone on the couch, leaned back, and closed his eyes. Whatever was going on in New Jersey, he was starting to dislike it because it began to involve people close to his heart. As he sat trying to put the pieces of the puzzle together, he found himself struggling to breathe.

He fought against the coil that had been wrapped and pulled tightly around his neck as it began to get tighter and tighter. He reach back to stop the attacker's assault but there was no one gripping the coil. That's when he realized it was a device programmed to do exactly what it was doing, strangle the life from its victims. Although he hadn't been able to defend himself against the assault, somehow his attacker walked around the couch and stood before him. "I thought you would like the last thing you saw to be the truth."

James' vision became blurred by tears along with the excruciating pain he was feeling. He stood to his feet and stumbled forward, as he reached his hand out. Before him there stood a clean-cut, six foot two, dark skin man dressed in navy blue slacks and a turtleneck, wearing latex gloves. The man politely moved to the side, allowing

James to crash to the floor. He clawed at the coil cutting into his throat until it was over.

Seeing the light diminish from his eyes, the attacker unlocked the device and removed it from James' lifeless corpse. He grabbed the cellphone off the couch and put it in his front pocket. With his mark eliminated, he exited the house the same way he'd entered. Undetected.

Back in his Land Rover, he called his contact.

"Uncle Mick, the weather is lovely in Patterson," the assassin said.

"Did you handle the package, Ken?" Mickey asked.

"Yes, that's taken care of," he replied.

"I appreciate that nephew. You understand why I couldn't handle it myself, right?" Mickey questioned.

"It's all good, man. That's what family is for. Besides, just make sure the money shows your appreciation," Ken said.

Mickey laughed. Not so much from humor but more so from the fact that he knew his nephew wasn't playing. Ken's demeanor, coupled with his clean-cut appearance, smoothness and youthfulness, would fool the average person.

James' mind flashed back to the last employer who had tried to pull a fast one on his nephew…

Kenneth Freeman, aka Malice, had rented the club for his 18th birthday. It was like a player's ball for mercenaries, big timers, and pimps. Silver Fox, one of the biggest pimps in Jersey, was having some issues with a detective who had fallen in love with one of his girls, so he'd asked around the professional hired-gun world for the best in the business. Hands down, everyone pointed him in Malice's direction.

Silver Fox had given him half of the ticket up front and promised the other fifteen thousand once the job was done. Unfortunately, the heat hit the strips his girls worked, due to the death of a detective and it hadn't been a coincidence. Malice had done the job sloppy purposely because he really disliked the prostitution world.

So when the time came for Silver Fox to pay him in full, he couldn't produce the check. He tried to send a few high dollar call-girls his way to work the debt off, but that wasn't Malice's style. On the other hand, he was a patient mercenary when it came to receiving his money. However, Silver Fox didn't know that quality about the youngster. Instead of being upfront, he got scared and tried the unthinkable— he tried to pay another mercenary to kill him.

Word reached his uncle through a reliable source and without hesitation, he called Malice and gave him the heads up. Of course, all he did was laugh before hanging up the phone.

The next day, Silver Fox, the call-girls, and the mercenary he'd propositioned were all found mutilated in a meat locker.

"Everything is business isn't it, Uncle James?" he asked for reassurance.

"Hold on," Mickey told him..

The guy on the other end of the line sent a text message to the employer, who texted back immediately with a screenshot showing the money transaction had been made. Mickey knew how his nephew was about sending certain messages to his phone, so rather than forward it he read the received text to him.

"Yeah, that's good business," Ken said. He let his Uncle know he was in traffic and told him he'd talk to him later.

After hanging up, he sat the phone on the charger and pulled up the iTunes icon. He pressed play on the only playlist he'd made, and the sounds of "Black Gloves" blared through the system, as he took the next exit heading to Newark, New Jersey.

***

Tabitha got her gear together and took a shower. Hearing the growl of her stomach, she snacked on a couple granola bars and some trail mix before heading out.

It was 6:15 pm when she pulled pull her uncle's driveway. As she stepped out of the car, an odd feeling suddenly came over her.

She approached the front door and noticed the house was completely quiet. With caution, she pulled the agency issued 40 Caliber GLOCK.

Easing the front door open, she walked in. "Uncle James are you ready to go?" she called out.

However, there was no reply. With every step, the sense of something being wrong became stronger. When she reached the den, her suspicions were confirmed by the sight before her.

"Uncle James!" She screamed as she rushed over to where his body lay stiff on the dark grey carpet. She would've checked his pulse but seeing the ring of congealed blood around his neck told her all she needed to know.

Through teary eyes, she called the police and reported the death of her uncle. They kept her on the line until the patrol cars and ambulance pulled up on the scene.

Running out to greet them, she met the officers and EMTs on the front porch. Before they could question her ties to the murder victim, she flashed her federal badge and stated her services to the federal government. From that moment on, they declined from asking her any questions based on her whereabouts, however, one of the officers did get a statement from her. They radioed for more backup and once the additional officers arrived, they put up the yellow crime scene tape.

Tabitha watched as the lifeless corpse of her uncle was covered by a white sheet and rolled out, before being pushed into the back of the ambulance.

Since he had been dead on arrival, EMT followed protocol and turned off the flashing lights and siren. She looked at the time and realized it was 8:15. Remembering she'd need to be in Jersey City the following afternoon, she put her personal feelings on hold and went to work.

Willie Slaughter

CHAPTER TWO

Tabitha checked into a hotel room at the agency's expense, so she treated herself to a luxurious suite. After another steamy hot shower to wash away the unnerving death of her Uncle James, she dressed in a dark green pantsuit and made her way to the office in Jersey City. Instead of driving, she took the Amtrak to give herself the time she needed to think about the course of action she was going to take concerning her uncle's death.

Since the young age of nine years old, he had been her only caretaker. After leaving their twelfth anniversary dinner, her mother and father had gotten killed in the crossfire of a gang shootout. According to the newspaper and news reports, it had been a bloody scene. They had called it *The Twelfth Anniversary Massacre*.

Besides the gangbangers who fled the scene, there had only been one sole survivor left. When the police arrived that night, she had lain across her mother's and father's bloody bodies, speechless. As fate would have it, one of the on-duty officers knew her uncle and called him. Every moment after that night, James Greene had been her mentor, guardian, and the only family she'd had to depend on.

The memories caused her eyelids to brim over with tears. Her determination to find out who killed him grew stronger by the second. She would treated his death the same way she'd treated her mother's and father's. It wasn't until after her uncle had trained her in seven of the deadliest forms of martial arts and taught her how to use any weapon at her disposal, that she'd been able to avenge her parents' death.

She remembered it as if it had happened just five minutes ago…

The New Jersey Devil Mob crew was having a neighborhood day celebrating their founding. From early day into nightfall, she pranced around in the neighborhood as if she lived there. Once nightfall set in, she changed into her midnight-blue assassin attire and began to commit murder after murder in some of the most hideous ways. The newspaper had referred to it as The Horrendous Murders: A Day of Retribution.

But what she did to their rivals, The Moneybag Gang, made their murders look like child's play. She had her uncle use his contacts to find each member's personal information. From house-to-house she went through like the angel of death, slaughtering everyone inside. Her thirst for vengeance had become so strong, he had to sit her down and remind her of the promises she'd made to end the rampage after the deaths of those responsible for the deaths of her parents.

Now, she was back to square one and her desire for vengeance had returned a hundredfold. Whoever was responsible for James' death would die in the most heinous way—that, she would make sure of.

When she looked up, she noticed a guy staring at her.

"Excuse me. Do I look familiar to you?" she asked irritated by his stare.

He smiled at her. "Actually, you do. But who knows? Everyone has multiple twins in this world."

"So you say," she replied.

"So I *know*, sister," he retorted.

"That's the first. So what's your aim?" she inquired, surprised by his choice of words.

He allowed himself to laugh. "Oh, a black man having some respect about himself is a rarity, huh? Well, my name is Kenneth, but my friends call me Ken."

Tabitha mustered up a smile. "Nice to meet you, Kenneth. I apologize; however, I don't give out personal information on sudden occasions. Maybe if I were to see you around on common ground every now and then I'd be more inclined to be friendly, although it's nothing personal against you."

Kenneth shrugged his shoulders. "No offense taken. We all have our moments."

The Amtrak stopped. The announcement of the destination was made over the loudspeaker and it was her stop. She headed for the exit and stopped at the open side door. When she turned around she looked him right in the eyes. "Thanks for understanding," she said, before turning to walk away.

She didn't wait for his reply but heard the faint sound of his voice telling her she was welcome anytime. She rode the escalator up onto the street, across from the federal building. She waited impatiently on the sidewalk signal to give the pedestrians the right of way to cross the street. After what seemed like thirty minutes, the signal turned green and everyone waiting to cross over hurried along.

Tabitha walked through the revolving door of the federal building. She gave her name and flashed her badge at the receptionist's desk. The scrawny, deeply-tanned, young woman put on her best smile.

"Director Wade Stevenson told me you would probably be here shortly. Right this way, Agent Greene," the secretary said.

Although she had seemed scrawny sitting behind the desk, Tabitha quickly noticed, moreover, the woman was a work of art. From her giddiness when mentioning the director's name, she also knew who was getting laid and possibly paid extra on the job.

The lady knew Tabitha was watching her, so she put some extra sway in her hips to add to the, already superb, sexuality she displayed naturally. Needless to say, that little move changed her whole outlook about the woman.

Feeling embarrassed, Tabitha stopped short in her steps. "Wait a second, ma'am. I owe you an apology."

"My name is Jennifer. Jennifer Humphrey, but go ahead. What's up?" the secretary replied.

Not knowing how he would take it, Tabitha had spent a lot of time trying to hide her down-low lifestyle from her uncle, and it felt a little odd to be upfront now, especially with a dime piece like Jennifer. About six foot one without the heels, she had long, braided, brunette hair and hazel brown eyes.

Tabitha looked into her eyes with the sincerest expression upon her face and sighed. . . "To be honest, in my mind, I automatically accused you of doing the director. I guess it was the enthusiasm in your voice when you said his name. The least I can do to make it up to you is buy you lunch or dinner maybe."

Jennifer didn't reply. She started walking again with a determining sway in her hips that said to Tabitha *'catch me if you can'*, and catching her was definitely something she had in mind. They reached the double doors which opened up to a conference room.

She held one side of the doors open to allow Tabitha to enter. Before she crossed the threshold, Jennifer put an arm up and blocked her path. She leaned into her arm letting the softness of her breast rub against it.

Jennifer smiled at her. "I'll see you after your meeting, Agent Greene. We'll talk about how you can make it up to me then."

"Okay," Tabitha replied.

She let her arm fall to her side and walked off as Tabitha proceeded to enter the room. For the most part, several top-secret agents sat around the table talking politics, some talked sports and family. Due to the wrinkles on his hands and face, and the hairpiece he wore to cover the balding grey, the director, who looked to be around fifty, sat quietly observing their interaction.

"Sir, Agent Tabitha Greene from Patterson, New Jersey." She introduced herself.

The chatter around the room ceased. The smiles and laughter from previous moments faded away. Their body postures and facial expressions transformed to that of strictly business. Director Wade Stevens stood and took center floor.

"It's nice having you with us, Agent Greene. As you know, I'm Director Wade Stevenson of the Jersey City division of the agency. To start from your left side and make my way around to your right, Agents Hailey Timmons, Timothy Barnes, Butch Henderson, Katherine Tolbert, Peter Sanders, Dominique Townsend, Saki Po, Amari Akoo, and Trinity Taiga."

Everyone nodded, and she returned the same gesture as a formal acknowledgement.

Director Stevens continued. "Everyone already knows why we're here, so let's get down to business. Things had been pretty quiet around here until these string of meat locker murders started. If it was left up to me, I'd probably rule the murders as justice served due to the caliber of people the victims were. However, good old Uncle Sam upstairs thinks differently, so here we are at the roundtable like knights about to seek justice for damned souls."

"Excuse me, Director Stevens," Agent Tolbert interjected.

Director Stevens looked at her. "Speak your mind, Agent Tolbert."

"What exactly are we expected to do here? From intel, there's no evidence that points to a generalized suspect. Who chases ghosts?" she asked.

The director nodded. "Damn good question, Agent Tolbert. At this table are the best agents New Jersey has given birth to. New Jersey also has a sinister underworld made of the finest of mercenaries. I'm not asking you to compromise your morality; however, you're being asked to go undercover and infiltrate the underworld to see what we come up with."

"And for how long is the operation afforded to last?" Agent Timmons asked.

"Agent Timmons, six weeks tops and we're pulling the plug. Not that we're pressed on funds, but statistically speaking, after six weeks if an operation hasn't produced concrete evidence someone, or should I say *some people* are bound to start slipping. And I don't want that someone or *people* to be any of you," Stevens replied.

Timmons nodded. "Fair enough."

Director Stevens slapped the top of the table. "Okay, pick you a partner if you choose to have one. If not, I understand, because being the best requires you to operate on your own, at your own pace."

No one picked a partner so once the meeting was adjourned, each person walked out solo. Director Stevenson had asked Tabitha to lag behind to speak with her privately. She obliged him.

"Agent Greene, I'm sorry to hear about your uncle. If there's anything I can do, just let me know," he said.

"He was the last of my family. I just need for him to have a proper burial and for him to be honored for his services to the United States Military." She responded sadly.

"No problem. I'll get right on it. And if you get even a little hunch on who you think could've done it, don't hesitate to contact me, and we'll take the son-of-a-bitch down for good," he said with confidence.

"My plans exactly. I'll keep you in mind, sir. Will that be all, sir?" she asked.

Director Stevens gave her a soldier's salute. "Carry on, Agent Greene."

She walked out of the conference. Jennifer was standing in front of the receptionist's desk looking like a supermodel in a sky-blue pinstripe skirt suit. Tabitha strolled over to where she stood and leaned against the desk. "Have you decided to accept my apology?"

"Do you like jazz, Agent Greene?" she asked smiling.

Tabitha smiled back at her. "It's one of my favorite genres. What's on your mind?"

"Dinner, at your expense, at a nice jazz spot I know three blocks from here," she replied.

"I'm game. Let me give you my number so you can call me and send me your address. I'll be by after I take a shower and dress for the occasion," Tabitha said. But by the look on Jennifer's face, she could sense she'd said something she may not have liked. She sighed, feeling somewhat frustrated. "What did I say wrong this time? I suppose I should've asked to read Jennifer's Manual before approaching you," she implied sarcastically.

That statement received a laugh and blush from Jennifer. "No silly. Where are you staying?"

"In a suite paid for by the job," she informed her.

Jennifer shook her head. "Nope, not anymore, babes. As long as you're in Jersey City, you're staying with me. So, let's go get your things and take them to my house.

That way we can both shower and get ready for our night out. It's not a problem is it?"

Tabitha looked surprised, but nonetheless, happy. "Not at all Jennifer." She looked at how the suit creased into her curvaceous body and could only imagine what she looked like beneath. "Not at all."

"Great. Let's go. My shift just ended," replied Jennifer.

They walked over and got on the elevator that led down to the parking garage. Luckily, they were alone because the two women found themselves staring into each other's eyes. Before either realized it, their hands were roaming, exploring the tender places on each other's body while their lips parted, allowing their tongues to intertwine in a passionate dance. The soft moans escaped from between both of their lips as the pleasure swelled between their thighs.

The bell sounding on the elevator signaling they had reached the parking garage floor brought them back to reality. They put some distance in between them—not out of shame, but out of understanding the things they were willing to do to each other regardless of where they were. The smiles on their faces said it all.

"Tabitha, I just need you to know one thing," Jennifer said.

"I'm listening," she replied, giving Jennifer her undivided attention.

"When it comes to my heart, I play for keeps. If this is just a game to you, let me know now; therefore, I'll know how far to think into this," Jennifer said seriously.

"Where's your car, Jenn? You'll find out soon enough, I'm not with the games," Tabitha said, with a straight face.

Jennifer pushed her against the wall of the elevator and kissed her passionately before they walked out of the elevator. She led Tabitha over to her charcoal grey 911 Porsche, that had the name Jennifer stenciled in burgundy paint across the trunk. Tabitha stood admiring the work of art while her newfound friend unlocked the doors.

They got in and when Jennifer started the car the engine purred like a kitten. "Let's ride, babes," she said. She pulled out of the garage and into the moving traffic. It was 5:13 pm, so traffic was at an average speed of 45 miles per hour. They listened to *Apple Cherry* while they rode through the downtown area passing the casino. The lyrics of the song reminded Tabitha of the taste of Jennifer's lips. The thought itself caused her to giggle.

"What's on your mind, Tabitha?" Jennifer asked.

"I see why you like this song. It's exactly how your lips taste," she replied.

Jennifer smiled. "So, what do you think the rest of me is tasting like?"

"If it gets any sweeter than your lips, I'm in trouble. I might lose control," Tabitha said seductively.

Jennifer bit her lower lip. "Mmm. . . I'm counting on it. By the way, how old are you?"

"19. And you?" Tabitha asked.

"26," Jennifer answered.

"The age difference isn't going to be a problem for you is it? I mean, we're going to see eye-to-eye versus you thinking everything has to be your way because of your age," Tabitha said.

"I'll only take charge when you seem to lose sight on what's important. Something I'll also expect you to do if I ever become emotionally imbalance. Fair?" she retorted.

Tabitha nodded in the affirmative and said, "I'm enjoying this relationship already."

"I am going to keep it that way," Jennifer said confidently.

They rode the rest of the way deep inside their own thoughts of one another.

Once they had made it to the hotel and inside the suite, she helped Tabitha pack her bags. Afterwards, Tabitha jumped on the bed and rolled over on to her back and stared into Jennifer's eyes. "It's sad I didn't get to sleep in this comfortable bed."

"You might not get the chance to sleep in it, but I have quite a few things in mind you can experience in it," Jennifer said flirtatiously.

"Jenn, you're speaking my language now, babes," Tabitha said smiling.

Tabitha unbuttoned her coat and blouse, and unsnapped her bra, revealing a perfect set of medium size breasts with freckles around the nipples.

Jennifer licked her lips as she mirrored Tabitha's action. Unbuttoning her top, her tan breasts were fully exposed and matched the rest of her smooth skin perfectly. "Come give me a kiss, sexy."

"Much obliged, babes," Tabitha replied.

She climbed onto the bed and lay beside her. They kissed and massaged each other's breasts until the nipples jutted out like pretty, bite size stud missiles. Used to being aggressive, Tabitha rolled over on top and began kissing and massaging her breasts, causing Jennifer to moan, sigh, and squirm beneath her. "Yummy, baby. You taste delicious," Tabitha whispered.

She continued to kiss all over her breasts, allowing her hand to roam freely and explore her body. She reached beneath Jennifer's skirt and pulled her thong to the side. Gently, she slid her fingers across her clitoris. She could feel her own heat rising within her, and her juices started to flow naturally, in response to the pleasure she administered. As Jennifer moaned and squirmed pressing her sexual organ up against her hand, Tabitha slowly slid two fingers inside her, while rubbing up and down on her clitoris with her thumb.

Jennifer clung to her like tomorrow wasn't promised while she made love to her with soft gentle strokes—one finger, then two, then three. . . She released again and again. With each release came a joyful sound to Tabitha's ears. Her body trembled and arched until Tabitha felt like she'd had given her enough for.

She kissed her way back up to her lips before getting up and straightening her clothes back out. She didn't take her eyes off of Jennifer's exposed breast and flat torso.

"Are you ready to go home now, babes?" Tabitha asked.

"Yes and no. I want to give you a dose of what you just gave me and more," was Jennifer's response.

"Aww, baby, thanks. You'll get your opportunity. Besides, my pleasure was in pleasing you. I was thinking about it the whole drive over," Tabitha said.

Jennifer stood and got herself together. They grabbed Tabitha's luggage, took the elevator down, and left the keys to the suite with the receptionist. Jennifer helped her put the luggage in the trunk before getting in her own car and taking the lead.

Thirty-seven minutes later, they pulled in her driveway.

The outside of the house looked great to Tabitha, but it couldn't compete with the inside. Artwork from different cultures aligned the walls, however, that wasn't the best part. A Jacuzzi sat inside a room surrounded by unlit candles, fresh incense burned in canters on the walls, and scented rose petals covered the floor.

"When was the last time this room was used?" Tabitha asked curiously.

Jennifer let out a sigh remembering the mistake she'd made loving a woman who didn't know how to deal with her affection. She'd come home from work and caught her and some hood chick making out in the Jacuzzi. She hadn't snapped right away, instead, she politely asked them to get out of her house, and they did.

Though, later on that evening, Jennifer had caught up with them and put two bullets in them. One in the heart for playing with her heart, and one in the head for playing with her mind. Giving Tabitha the tour of her house was the first time she'd opened the door since then.

"It's been awhile," Jennifer said, shaking the events of that night away from her mind.

"We're going to change that, Jenn," Tabitha said reassuringly.

"I hope so, babes. But for now, let's get you settled in, so we can shower and have our night out on you." Jennifer smiled. Her heart felt happier than it had in a while and she was elated Tabitha had crossed her path.

"On me?" Tabitha said, pointing at herself.

Jennifer laughed while nodding. "Yep. You offered me dinner, and I'm definitely not declining the offer."

"I'm a babe of her word," Tabitha replied.

She unpacked and joined Jennifer in the shower.

Seeing each other's flawless nude bodies caused them to begin exploring one another with their hands, eyes, and lips. They kissed and rubbed body-to-body until their hunger for one another subsided.

After bathing one another, they got out of the shower and dried off. Realizing they would never make it to dinner if they attempted dressed in the same room, Tabitha grabbed her clothes and walked to another room to finish getting dressed.

The two ladies stepped out dressed to impress. Jennifer, in her powder blue Ralph Lauren body dress, and Tabitha in a lime green Nautica cat suit. Deciding to take the Porsche, they reached the jazz spot in the downtown area a little after 9 pm.

CHAPTER THREE

Without knowing each other's strategy, Agents Barnes, Sanders, and Townsend had been thinking along the same lines. Coincidentally, they'd all ended up at one of the hottest underground hangout spots in Jersey City. Playing it smart, neither approached the other, but instead played the complete stranger role to maintain their covers.

The party was live. Players, both men and women of different age groups, strutted through in their high dollar attire and jewelry. The pimps hit the aisles showboating their topnotch call-girls and boys. It was a real tell-tale party.

Timothy Barnes sat at the bar sipping on a Long Island Iced Tea, when one of the sexiest call-girls in the room sat in the barstool on his right. She pretended to be into the soccer game on the TV, posted on the wall behind the bar. When it came to call-girls, Timothy knew the game all too well and he was always willing to play along to curb his sexual appetite.

"Excuse me, bartender!" he yelled.

The clean shaved olive skin man looked over his shoulder as he continued buffing the shot glass. He was an easy six-four in height and two hundred ninety, solid in weight.

"Get the young lady a tequila on me!" he said.

Using the same glass, he poured the shot of tequila and sat it in front of her. Timothy observed her body language out of his peripheral vision. She continued to watch the game without even touching the drink. A little irritated by her nonchalant attitude, he swerved around on the rotatable barstool to face her. "Hi. My name is Tim."

"I'm Angela, but my friends call me Angel," she replied.

When she didn't bother to look at him, it donned on him that maybe she was really into soccer game. The muscle tone within her arms and calves were deeply defined. *Maybe I made a mistake by buying her the drink,* he thought.

"I apologize if I offended you by buying you a drink. I was just trying to be polite." He apologized.

"No, you were just trying to pay a little extra for a good time with a call-girl," she responded sarcastically.

He rubbed the back of his neck. It was something he always did when he'd been made.

She realized it, and smirked. "You're a terrible liar, Tim."

"You're a beautiful angel, Angel. I take it you're not a call-girl?" he asked.

She spun around facing him for the first time since the conversation started. Her expression went from a cool smile to a cold calculated unnerving one, which made him shift a little on the stool. Realizing she wasn't going to drink the shot of tequila, he reached for it, but his movement was too fast for her liking.

Within a split-second, she caught him by the wrist, twisted it while pulling him towards her, and, in her free hand, a two-inch Shadow Dagger mysteriously appeared, and the blade was at his throat.

"No, I'm not a call-girl. I don't fuck for fun, funds or free. If I'm with you, then I'm with you. If not—" She pricked his skin with the tip of the dagger, causing a small bead of blood to surface. "Well, you get the picture."

Through his wrist she could feel the change in his heart rate, and what she felt was fear. Something she'd expected. His type was something she knew all too well.

Her father was his type. Preyed on the weakness of the mind to conquer the heart and subject it to bleed for him only. Her mother had been one of his many victims—a victim who paid with her life.

Angela found herself treading down memory lane. . .

There she was, at the age of 16, a rising star on the high school's soccer team. The captain of the team to be exact. It was the championship game, and she'd scored the game-winning goal due to a penalty kick.

After the game, the coaches threw the team the party of their lifetime. She'd been proclaimed MVP and given the trophy and medal to tell the story. Her mother was all smiles, proud of her. She enjoyed the moment shared between them silently more than the party itself.

After the party, they took the Amtrak home. They talked and laughed the entire ride. When they arrived home, the happiness dissolved into fear. Her father was drunk, and every time he drank, violence was sure to follow.

Usually, he would have the decency to give her time to shower and get in bed, but not this time. He had beat her mother to death right in front of her. The shock of the moment had worn off of her too late to save her mother,

37

but not too late to save herself. She knew where the gun was stashed, and quickly ran to retrieve it. When he walked in the room, she emptied the clip into him.

He could tell something was deeply disturbing her because of the emotional reaction it triggered. He still didn't attempt to make any sudden movement.

"Listen Angel, I was only reaching for the drink that you aren't drinking. So, could you please calm your nerves?" he said apprehensively.

She closed her eyes to fight back the tears. After a few moments had passed, she took a deep breath, opened her eyes, and decided to let him live.

Once she released his wrist and sheathed the dagger, he grabbed the shot of tequila and downed it in one gulp. He sat the glass down and ordered another shot to sooth his nerves.

"Excuse me, Tim. It was nice meeting you, but I have to go. Enjoy the party," she said.

She got up and walked off. He watched her go. The way her hips swayed beneath the spandex smoke grey pants had him hypnotized.

"She's a work of art, my man. Unfortunately, that's out of your league," said a male's voice beside him.

Tim turned to see who the voice belonged to and it turned out to be a well-dressed, medium build, clean shaved, brown skin man, sporting a protective look on his face.

"Well, I don't know about the *out of my league part*, but she's a real looker," he said, and put his hand out, "the name is Tim."

The guy looked at his hand and back into his eyes. "Are you really so friendly that you give everyone you meet such important information Tim?"

The man made it obvious he wasn't going to shake his hand, so Tim let his hand rest on the edge of the bar. "I wouldn't consider me being friendly. I'm just an outgoing people-person who gives everyone the benefit of the doubt."

The guy smirked. "So you say. Bartender, pour him a drink of your best and put it on my tab."

The bartender's only response was to pour the drink and walk down to the opposite end of the bar.

Timothy downed the shot and grimaced as it burned going down. "Phew! That's a stiff one. Thanks, my man."

"No problem, Tim. Words from the wise, don't mess with my little sister. Enjoy the rest of the party," the man said, before he eased off the barstool and left.

***

Agent Sanders didn't approach Agent Barnes, but he definitely had him in his sight. More so out of the habit of feeling the need to have a fellow agent's back. The party was proving to be therapeutic for him. Since his fiancé had died, he hadn't gotten out much. Not so much from the fact she died, but because of the *way* she died.

It was at their engagement party. They were surrounded by family and friends. Everyone was having a ball until the doorbell rang. And in stepped his ex-girlfriend.

He should've known something was wrong by the tears in her eyes. Before he could process what was happening, she revealed the gun she'd held behind her back, and opened fire. Her aim was nothing less than perfect. Each bullet struck the chest of his fiancé ending his happiness.

"Trip down memory lane?" a lady walked up to him and said. "I do the same thing every now and then. More than I would like to. I guess we all have our angels and demons." The unfamiliar feminine voice coached him back to reality.

He looked up into the face of the woman standing directly in front of him. She was an above average redhead dressed so every man's desire would be to undress her. Her cool mannerism spoke volumes to him about the caliber of woman before him.

"If you're selling, I'm not interested. I'm just having a quiet night out," said Agent Sanders.

"If you were trying to buy me, you would realize I'm not for sale. Every good-looking woman at this party isn't a slave, nor are they all selling their bodies. Don't get me wrong, we can all find ourselves enslaved to something, or someone, if we're not careful," the woman replied.

"You can say that again," he said, while extending his hand. "Pete's the name. How're you doing?"

She looked at his outstretched hand. "Pete, I don't kiss and tell. That's a dangerous game for a fool. I saw you making an attempt to escape reality and decided to help you find your way back to serving your purpose. Now that I've accomplished my mission, enjoy the remainder of the evening."

She turned around and sashayed off, leaving him to process what she'd said.

***

Agent Townsend had observed her fellow agents get dissed by the women. The first one with Barnes caused her to laugh. The woman had class and skills, not to mention a brother who pulled up right after and, to her, laid down the law.

The women gave her a sense of pride in being a woman, especially being a 34-year-old black woman. Life had been full of pain and hardship for her. Her mother had overdosed on heroin after her father had left them for a call-girl. It wasn't long afterwards when he was found washed up on the shore with two holes in his skull.

That happened when she was 14. Since then, she had lived with her mother's side of the family, and they'd groomed her for success.

"Look like you could use some great company. Do you mind?"

She shook off the memory. The guy standing to her left was tall, dark and handsome. The shining bald head and neatly groomed beard added to his handsomeness.

Agent Townsend smiled up at him. "I don't mind at all. Have a seat." She slid her chair around to face him.

He nodded, admiring her manners. "Are you having a secret assessment party going on that I need to be aware of?"

"Something to that nature. My perception of you is straight forward. You prefer to look every challenge in the eyes versus putting your focus on your own two feet," she replied.

"Well, I stand on them every day, but I'm not approached by you every day. So, it's best to pay attention to what's before you at all times because the mirror will definitely reveal what's behind you," he responded, and got up and walked off.

At first, she thought she'd run him off, possibly, good company and a good companion, until he returned carrying two drinks and a plate of deep-fried potato wedges smothered in honey mustard sauce. He sat everything down on the table.

"Your reward for giving me the best conversation ever," he complimented her.

She picked up one of the potato wedges and bit into it. "Mmm, this is delicious. Thanks," she said, and went to work on the rest of the potato wedges.

He watched amusingly. "You're welcome my sister. Anytime."

"My name is Dominique. And don't make any promises you can't keep mister," she retorted.

He denied himself the laughter he felt inside, but not the smile. "I'll make a mental note of that. I'm Trent."

They sat and chat until the party started quieting down and people started leaving. She finished off the potato wedges and reached for the drink. When she realized she'd gotten the sauce all over her fingers, he noticed as well as she looked around for a napkin.

"May I?" Trent asked. He grabbed her hand and slowly licked her fingers clean of the sweet tasting sauce. He moaned, savoring the taste while looking into her dark brown eyes.

She could no longer sit still. Her body had developed a mind of its own, and it was demanding her to give in to the pleasures it sought from him.

"Alright, smooth operator, I hope you know what you're doing," Dominique said.

"There's only one way to find out black queen," he replied, staring into her eyes.

He took her by the hand and led her through the dimly lit room. They entered a room which was fully furnished with a queen size bed in the center. He placed kisses around her earlobes and neck while undressing her from behind. She sighed and allowed herself to relax, giving him full control.

Once he had undressed her fully, he turned her around to face him, before taking a step backwards to get the full view of her body. The sight before him caused his manhood to ache from the hardness. Her whole body was perfectly toned and soft to the touch.

Next, he undressed himself and took her into his embrace.

Together, they fell onto the bed which Dominique instantly realized was a waterbed. They rode the waves to ecstasy. Her climax came so strong, she wrapped her legs around his waist and arched her back, pulling his phallus deeper inside until their juices ceased to flow.

"I hope you don't think any less of me than you did an hour or so ago," she said, feeling a little ashamed for giving into her cravings without really knowing him.

"And why would I do that, Dominique?" he asked.

Without answering, she reached for her clothing and he followed suit. Once they finished dressing, he pulled her into a longing kiss and she melted into it without hesitation.

She pulled back and smiled. "Point taken," she said, "but when will I see you again?"

He held out his hand. And assuming why, she handed him her personal cellphone. He typed in his phone number and additional contact information and gave it back.

"I'm just a telephone call away, beautiful," he said sincerely.

They walked out into the cool night air. He walked her to her car and opened the door.

"Such a gentleman," she said, complimenting him just as he'd done her earlier.

"Well, there's always two sides to every coin. You just so happen to receive the winning toss. I'll see you again soon, hopefully. Until then, stay you." Trent responded like the suave man he was.

Dominique smiled, staring into his eyes. "That's all I can do."

He shut the door and watched as she drove off.

CHAPTER FOUR

Tabitha woke up the next morning, to Jennifer sound asleep in her arms. The previous night had been majestic, and she was feeling anew. She got up and began her usual routine—a light stretch, workout, and a thirty-minute yoga session. She was so into it she didn't notice Jennifer watching.

"I would've loved doing your routine with you, Tabby," Jennifer said.

She jumped to her feet smiling from ear to ear. "It's cool, Jenn. Besides, you were looking so beautiful while sleeping, there's no way I could've disturbed you. But now that you're up, let's have breakfast, and to work we go."

"Why can't I just have you for my buffet?" Jennifer pouted.

"Aww baby, give me some lip," Tabitha told her.

They kissed as Jennifer sat up and got out of the bed. Subsequently, they took a quick shower together before eating breakfast.

Since the two were heading to the same location, they took the Audi 8. Tabitha parked in the parking garage and informed Jennifer she would be working until 10 pm.

"Well, I'll take the Amtrak home. You keep the car," Jennifer said.

Tabitha took the key out of the ignition and slid them inside Jennifer's pocket as she kissed her. "No, you won't. I'll see you when I get home tonight."

She didn't give Jennifer time to respond. She opened the car door, got out, and began at a trot through the parking garage.

Jennifer stood next to the car and watched her until she turned the corner and into the daylight. Thinking about how things were turning out, she smiled, strolled over to the elevator, and rode to the conference floor.

***

The early morning hours were his best hours, but not the hours he liked best. Malice removed the corpses, putting them with the third one on the meat grinder line, inside the slaughterhouse. After they became ground up meat and bone, Angel mopped up the blood while everyone else wiped everything down. With the corpses disposed of, they took turns in the hot shower.

Malice was the last to shower. He stepped out dressed in dark grey slacks and a black turtleneck. Everyone else sat around breaking down, oiling, and grooving the barrels of guns, and sharpening daggers, knives and swords.

The previous night, Malice had been at the party playing the shadows and watching the team run interference while business was being conducted. The business that resulted in the three corpses becoming chopped meat for the creatures of the water.

"What did everyone learn from last night's drill?" he asked, looking from one face to another.

"Either they've sent the dumbest agents undercover or they're smart enough to keep cool while in a den of lions.

Especially the one I approached. I believe he said his name was Tim," Angel said sarcastically.

"You talking about this guy?" Malice asked, as he tossed the pictures on the table. They had all seen the marks they had dealt with at the party.

Angel stop polishing her Dragon Daggers and looked at the pictures on the table. "Yeah, that's him. Tim."

"Short for Timothy. Timothy Barnes to be exact. A known federal agent," Malice said.

She resumed polishing her blades. "I guess we'll have to see if his reputation proceeds itself. May I?"

"Angel, when have mercenaries ever needed permission to be a mercenary? My only concern is, we keep everything evidence free," Malice replied.

Trent stared at the picture of Dominique Townsend. His thoughts immediately took him to the memory of their private after the party, the intimate moment they'd shared. The taste and feel of her soft body . . . Her passion was a luxurious gift from the Gods to him.

The memory caused him to swear silently. As long as she didn't press hard to do her job, she would live, and they would continue to have their moments. *It's the least I can do*, he thought to himself.

The other two agents were as good as dead. Angel and Valencia had already marked them.

Malice's thoughts went back to the woman he'd met on the Amtrak. He wondered when, if ever, he would see her again. "All I can say is, do what you do best. We're family, and nothing comes between family. We live and kill together. We all have things to do, so we'll meet up later," he reminded them.

Everyone got up and made their exit.

Malice found himself in the uptown area at a drama club watching the actors and actresses perform. It was his daily amusement to see people be swift and changeable in personality. Kind of reminded him of himself. As the show neared to his favorite performances of the spoken words play script, he noticed her sitting on the front row.

His body reacted before his mind could second-guess his actions, and next thing he knew, he was sitting beside her. Neither said a word during the performance, and after the stage cleared, without saying a word, Tabitha got up to leave.

"You're a very unfriendly woman you know," Kenneth said, staring nonchalantly at the empty stage.

She stopped and sighed heavenward. "Kenneth is it?"

He stood up and performed a gentleman's bow. "At your service ma'am."

"You seem to be a pretty good judge of character, Kenneth, so you know when a woman has other preferences," she said coolly.

"You're correct. But whoever said I was out to wife you or anything of the sort? Can't a guy seek a genuine friendship without thinking below the waist? Don't get me wrong, you're a beautiful young sister; however, like you, I don't believe in trying to force things in places it doesn't fit in," he replied.

Tabitha nodded. "Understood. Well, I see you have found a common ground. Now I'm wondering how close you've been following me lately."

Her sense of humor deserved to be rewarded, so he allowed himself to laugh and followed up with a smile— two things he really didn't care too much for. "Unfortunately, I haven't been as close as I would like to be. There's something special about you."

She checked the time. It was a little after 9 am, a great time for her to hit the gym and go a couple rounds in the ring and with the bags. "Listen Kenneth, my life is built around a very tight schedule. Like right now is my training time, and it doesn't look like you're dressed to jog to the gym and go a few rounds with me."

Kenneth frowned. "Is that prejudgment I'm hearing? Lead the way champ."

They exited the building. Without fair warning, Tabitha took off jogging. His long stride caught him up real fast.

"Boy, you surely don't play by the rules," he said, as he jogged alongside her.

"Kenneth, you've lived long enough to know you must be prepared at all times. Reaction time is a difference maker between life and death," Tabitha replied.

To him, according to his own philosophy and the principles he lived by, hers was very admirable. They jogged the rest of the way silently, at a sprinter's pace.

They stopped and caught their breath outside, in front of the gym . She nodded showing a newfound respect for him.

"Not bad, Kenneth."

He chuckled. "Oh, you haven't seen anything yet, sis."

"Is that a challenge? Because I enjoy a good challenge," she said.

He grabbed the door and pulled it open. "After you."

They entered the gym and did a little warmup exercise and stretch before getting in the ring. The owner offered them headgear, mouth guards, and gloves, but Tabitha declined.

"Are you sure you don't want to gear up?" asked Kenneth.

She ignored the question. Her expression was blank while taking off her shoes and socks. Seeing she was ready for more action than conversation, he came out of his shoes, socks, and shirt. The smirk on her face was priceless.

"The cover of the book looks good. Let's see how the mechanics are. Shall we?" she asked.

He went into a forward fold stretch. "What style, sis?"

"Call me Tab. And choose your favorite. I'll compensate," she answered.

"Okay, Tab. Full contact or are we pulling punches?" he asked.

"This time, we'll pull. But all throws and takedowns are full throttle," she answered.

Everyone in the gym had gathered around the ring. One of the fighters set the match clock for five-minute rounds and rang the bell.

They circled around each other in the ring. Remembering what her Uncle James had taught her about knowing the difference between a skilled fighter and one who was untrained, she flexed as if she was launching an attack, and when he didn't flinch, she changed up her style.

"From judo to jujitsu. Nice, Tab," Kenneth said admiringly. He smiled, and as he was about to switch styles himself, she tucked and rolled on the mat, and caught him off guard with an arm leg sweep. He hit the mat, back first. Before she could get a firm grip on his leg, he rolled left and sprung back to his feet.

"Alright. You're not an amateur. I'll give you that," he said.

The fighters around the ring cheered her on. He pretended to get distracted by turning his back to her, talking to the onlookers in his corner. Tabitha saw it as the perfect opportunity for a submission hold. She decided to go low again, but this time with a grappling maneuver. What she didn't know was, it was exactly what he'd anticipated.

As she reached for his legs, he spun around and stunned her with a knee roundhouse to the chin. While still in motion, he flipped over her back and rolled her on over to the mat into a lumbar submission hold. She tapped to submit. He let go of her arm and stood up.

"You jammed on me, Ken," she said. She remained on the mat. He noticed she had called him by the alias he'd told her all his friends use.

"It was highly anticipated, Tab. You did exactly what any good fighter would've done. Unfortunately, it only works if the opponent isn't giving you an illusion to attack," he responded.

She smiled, and as he made an attempt to assist her in getting up, she spun around, braced her body with her hands and swept him off his feet. He watched from the mat as she performed the Brazilian art to the tee and flipped to her feet.

"Okay, Miss Brazil. Expect the unexpected," was his response to Tabitha's maneuver.

Their audience clapped and whistled loudly. He stood up, they faced each other, and bowed. He hit the men's shower while she hit the lady's. He finished and waited on her at the bar, drinking an orange juice.

"Hey man, are you waiting on the lady you sparred with?" one of the boxers asked him.

"Yeah. Why you ask?" Kenneth replied with a question of his own.

Still sporting wraps around his fists and wearing the headgear, the man started laughing. That irritated Kenneth.

"Son, your game must be on ice. She left about five minutes before you got out the shower. You gotta tap something like that right, son," the young man said jokingly.

Now his anger was getting the best of him. The guy was well built and probably had half of a decent fight game, but Kenneth had already sized him up three ways. His weight, clothes size, and the casket someone would be burying his corpse in. Actually, not would be, but *will* be, because he'd already made his mind up to send him to meet his maker.

"Yo' son, you got mad skills. Maybe you can give me some extra lessons," the man said.

That played right into his thoughts. He took down the fighter's information and left.

***

Agents Timmons, Henderson, and Tolbert found themselves sitting in the casino early. Initially, nobody wanted to do the partnership, but seeing as how the wild goose chase seemed to be just that, they decided to link up and have a little fun while they were undercover. They appeared to be a group of high rollers out for some early afternoon fun at the craps table. Fortunately, as luck would have it, they hit some pretty good licks.

Dressed in a double-breasted tan Armani suit, a middle-aged guy around five foot eight, with dark brown skin and wavy hair, walked over to the table and stood cross from them. Shortly afterwards, a balding Caucasian man about the same height and build came over and sat next to him. He whispered something in the middle-aged guy's left ear. All the same, his focus never diverted from them. He could tell that his presence, along with the curiosity of not knowing what he'd just been told, made the man accompanying the two ladies uncomfortable.

"Say, my man, you play poker?" the man asked.

"Name the game, big timer," Henderson replied.

The stranger rubbed his palms together. "Mickey's the name, my man. And I play for keeps, so Straight poker is the game."

"What's the wager, Mickey? And, by the way, the name is Butch," he countered.

Mickey tapped the table, imitating the beat of a drum roll. The gamer quickly removed the dice and pulled out a brand-new deck of Bicycle Playing Cards. "Three hundred a stay, a hundred every check, and nothing under five hundred raises. Cool?"

Butch nodded. "Count me in. Is your buddy playing?"

Mickey shook his head. "No. It's just me and you, Butch. One of us will walk away a wealthy man."

Both men asked for ten thousand in poker chips.

Mickey eyed the two women standing on opposite sides of Henderson. Neither were what he considered high dollar, nonetheless, both were doable. "I see you've got your lucky charms with you," he said, "maybe for more than just winning currency."

"Yeah, and so far so good, Mickey," Butch answered, picking up on the sarcasm.

Mickey nodded towards the dealer, a prompt to empty the deck onto the table. He mixed the cards facedown before collecting and shuffling them. The men watched as the dealer stopped shuffling and cut the cards.

"Alright, gentlemen, place your bets. The game is Five-card draw. No Hi-Lo. Straight poker. Meaning, you play what you get and what turns out on the table. Understood?" the dealer asked.

Both men nodded. Their eyes stayed locked on one another while the dealer dealt their hands. Before looking at the five cards faced down before them, each player slid a total of six hundred in poker chips to the center of the green carpeted table.

Without batting an eye, Butch picked up the five cards, never once looking away from Mickey. He noticed Mickey hadn't even bothered to look at his hand.

Mickey sat across the table displaying the straightest poker game-face he'd ever seen. And he knew he had Butch shaken up. "What will it be, my man?" he asked.

Butch tossed another hundred on the pile. "Check."

The dealer flipped over three of the five cards near the center of the table. Mickey looked at the deuce of hearts, jack of spades, and ten of diamonds.

"You know the beauty is in the unknown, Butch. A gamble is never a thing of certainty unless the game is already rigged to your favor. Check," Mickey said, before he tossed a hundred onto the pile. "So, what's it going to be, my man?"

Butch looked at his hand again. From the layout, he was looking at two pairs, king-high. But then again, there were the other two facedown cards which could possibly give him a boat, jacks over tens. He pushed five hundred to the pile of poker chips, causing his opponent to smile.

"I see your raise, and I raise the wager another five," Mickey responded with a smile.

He's either a big timer who lives for the excitement of a good gamble, or he's crazy, Butch thought to himself. He honored his raise.

"Check." He tossed another hundred into the pot.

The dealer flipped over a card. It was the nine of clubs. Mickey tossed in his hundred.

"Are you really a gambling man, Butch? Check," Mickey said.

He tossed another hundred, and the dealer flipped the last card. It was the seven of spades.

"Alright, gentlemen, all cards have been revealed. Now, the game belongs to you," said the dealer.

Although Butch was nervous, he didn't let it show. At least he thought he didn't, but Mickey saw straight through the illusion. He picked up two thousand dollars' worth of poker chips and dropped them, one at a time, onto the pile while staring into Butch's eyes. "What is it you see in the mirror, Butch? Are you confident in your hand?"

If his intention was to bait him up, it definitely worked. He accepted the raise and raised another five hundred to go with the two thousand. "I take my chances. Like you said, there's no certainty in a gamble."

Mickey pushed five hundred to the center. "Call, my man."

Butch revealed his hand. "Two pairs. Jacks over tens king-high."

"Hmm. . . Not bad. Not bad at all," Mickey commented. For the first time since the game had begun, he peaked at the five cards before him. "But, not good enough." He flipped the cards over one at a time. "Seven, eight, nine, ten, jack. Straight."

The dealer raked the pile of poker chips over to Mickey's side of the table. "We have a winner. Straight beats two pairs," he announced. He turned the deck of cards face-up on the table to show both men the deck hadn't been a mole deck. Sensing both men were satisfied with the confirmation, he turned the cards back over and mixed them up.

"Will you gentlemen be playing another game?" he asked.

Butch looked at his watch. It was going on 2 pm. Nothing was looking suspicious, and he wasn't trying to leave broke. It was very clear to him, Mickey had long money, something he didn't have.

"Mickey, my man, today was your lucky day, tomorrow might not be. Until then, enjoy your winnings. Now, if you all would excuse us, my company and I must get going," Butch said.

Butch and his fellow agents had been so focused on the poker game, nobody considered paying attention to the rest of the environment— that's how the armed men dressed in jet black suits ended up posted right behind them. As soon as he tried to stand, a hand gripped his right shoulder and forced him back down onto the chair.

"What's going on, Mick?" Butch questioned him. He knew he'd been caught slipping.

"Mick is something my friends call me, and men like me don't have many friends, Agent Henderson," he answered in a nonchalant manner. He could smell the fear coming from him.

Their cover was blown. The three agents assessed the situation in their own way. Timmons and Tolbert did what came natural. They played double agents, cussing him for jeopardizing their lives by not letting them know he was a federal agent.

"The way I see it, Butch Henderson, what's yours is already mines," Mickey told him.

It wasn't like he didn't know the two women were federal agents as well, but he let them play the part. "Well ladies and gentlemen, it's time we take a stroll."

The dealer collected the poker chips and casually walked off, not caring to be a witness to too much of anything. The armed men searched the three agents. Due to house rules, they weren't carrying.

They escorted the trio out the rear entrance at gunpoint. It surprised Butch to see the trunk of his Dodge Charger open.

"Get in the trunk, agent. And don't make me tell you twice," Mickey demanded.

He complied, realizing his life was possibly over. He only hoped the ladies would be spared. But something told him their futures would also be nonexistent.

"Now, for the moment of truth," Mickey declared. He nodded to one of his gunmen. The gunmen took the cue and pulled out two Berettas and handed them over to Timmons and Tolbert. Mickey pointed towards Butch, who now lay in the trunk, and said, "This guy, Federal Agent Henderson, just endangered your lives. If that's the true case, you have the opportunity to do unto him as he would've allowed to be done unto you without remorse. And all for the sake of Uncle Sam, might I add."

Hailey hesitated, but Katherine didn't. She unloaded the clip into him. She made an attempt to hand the gun back to the gunman, but he told her to keep it.

Mickey smiled, admiring Katherine's handy work. "Now, here's my speculation . . . either you're a heartless woman, with no sense of loyalty, and she's an agent like her dead friend, or both of you are agents. Or does one just value life more than the other?" he asked, looking at Katherine then Hailey.

Grabbing another gun from the gunman's holster, Katherine swung around expertly and shot Hailey twice in the chest and once in the head. Two of the guards picked the body up and tossed her in the trunk.

Mickey spun around and looked her up and down, admiring her strong will to live. "What's your name?"

"Katherine Tolbert," she answered.

"Can I hire your services, Miss Tolbert? I promise you'll make more in a week than what you're clocking in a year. What do you say killer?" he asked.

"Count me in," she responded quickly.

He closed the trunk just as three of his men got in another car and drove off. He and Katherine continued discussing all the requirements she'd need to be on his team.

Willie Slaughter

CHAPTER FIVE

By now, Tabitha had worked her way around the streets of Jersey City. Due to the background she'd come from, it was easy. She spoke the lingo, when necessary, and she knew the codes. Still, there wasn't any talk going around about the meat locker murders.

As she started to backtrack, the hairs on her arms stood up. Immediately, she knew someone was either following her or watching her closely. Regardless, the feeling was of ill intent. She took to the back streets to see if whoever it was would be stupid enough to give up their cover by following her into the alley.

To her amusement, a short, stocky masculine figure dressed in dark clothing stepped into the alleyway behind her. As far as she could tell he didn't have a weapon in his hand, so she played the terrified damsel-in-distress role.

Facing him, she started treading backwards as she spoke in a panicked tone, "I don't have much money. I'm poor and I have two little girls at home. Please, don't hurt me."

She watched as the guy took out his phone and looked at the screen. It was obvious he was studying a picture, a picture most likely of her. When he put the phone back inside his jacket pocket and proceeded to continue moving towards her, her suspicion was confirmed.

She slowed her pace, preparing herself to attack. All of a sudden, another figure dressed in dark clothing entered the alleyway behind the first man. She kept her eyes on the short guy in front who hadn't paid attention to the figure creeping up on him at a fast pace. Although the alleyway was quiet, she could still hear the footsteps of the second man gaining on the rear of her attacker.

He was almost in striking distance when she saw the glint of the steel as it was being unsheathed by the figure bringing up the rear. The blade of the sword went through his back and became visible on the front side. The figure twisted the hilt deep inside him causing the blade to sever columns of the spine, while exerting internal damage. He snatched it out of him swiftly. And although the guy was dead before he hit the ground, the figure beheaded him without remorse.

Instead of approaching her, the mysterious figure scaled the fire escape stairwell and disappeared in the shadows. It wasn't until that moment that Tabitha realized whoever it was had been wearing a navy-blue ninja suit.

Okay then, she thought out loud. She walked over to the beheaded corpse and searched him. She took his cellphone but left everything else. She didn't call the police, because it would've been hard to explain how a ninja had come to her rescue. Having had enough for one night, she trotted down into the terminal and got on the Amtrak.

Once Tabitha had finally made it to her destination, she looked at the house and sighed. The lights were off so she figured Jennifer must've been asleep. But, to her surprise, she wasn't. She actually greeted her with a kiss at the front door and then helped her undress.

"Tabby, you seem a little tense. Let's get you comfy so you can relax. I have just the thing," Jennifer said.

She led her by the hand and into the Jacuzzi room. She had already planned the moment, so the candles and incense had been lit, giving off a sweet aroma that started working on Tabitha's mind instantly. Jennifer allowed the hot pink lingerie she was wearing to drop to the floor, and together, they eased into the warmth of the Jacuzzi.

At first, they sat in silence and Jennifer noticed Tabitha deeply in thought.

"Tabby, no secrets no lies. What's wrong?" she pried.

Tabitha maneuvered around in the water until she had Jennifer within her embrace. She brushed her hair to the side and kissed her on the nape of her neck. She responded by relaxing her body and leaning back onto her.

"Jenn, I didn't know Jersey had ninjas," Tabitha said.

She giggled, thinking Tabitha was just being her crazy, humorous self. But, when she realized it wasn't a hee-hee ha-ha moment, her face became a reflection of her confusion. "Are you saying you saw a ninja, or are you saying you were attacked by a ninja, babes? Because I didn't know we had ninjas either. Maybe Chinatown decided to show some cultural history."

Tabitha shook her head. "No, the ninja didn't attack me. He actually came to my rescue." She went on to tell Jennifer about the whole alleyway incident.

Jennifer had an uneasy feeling and pressed her body even closer against Tabitha's.

"I got the perp's cellphone. I figured we could have the data log investigated. Maybe it'll shine a light on who's out to bury me," she said.

"Well, with ninjas on our team, burying you is the last thing I'm concerned about. My concern is the fact that this person or *ninja* has your identification, so that means there's a mole in agency. We can't trust them. I have data analyzer software on one of the computers in the den. We'll check it out tomorrow evening after work," Jennifer replied.

"Jenn," she said.

"What, Tabby," Jennifer replied.

"It's obvious you don't want me staying out late night. Just say it," Tabitha told her.

"I truly don't. Especially with that kind of activity going on," she answered honestly.

"Jenn," Tabitha said again.

"Yes, hon," she answered.

"I love you," Tabitha said.

"I love you too, Tabby."

The two kissed and made out in the Jacuzzi before going to bed.

***

Malice was on his way in for the night when he remembered the promise he'd made death, concerning a certain soul. He ran, jumping from rooftop to rooftop, a shadow pitched against the night. He knew the city like the back of his hand. He crouched low on the rooftop across from the apartment of his target. Observing the movement inside, he made sure not to miss the flow of traffic below.

The fighter appeared to be having a good time. He bobbed his head, rocking to the beat and lyrics of *Stand Up*.

Malice watched as the young man entered the kitchen, grabbed two beers from the fridge, and bopped back into the living room, where his company sat. Judging by the way she was dressed, he could tell she was a call-girl. They talked and casually sipped the beers which caused him to smirk. *What's up with all the role-play? Whatever happened to pay, handle your business, and give them the boot?* Malice thought to himself.

Finally, the moment he'd patiently been waiting on had arrived. The lights went out and he made his move. Without making a sound, he entered the apartment through the kitchen window and moved silently and swiftly through the hallway. He stood at the open door of the bedroom. Listening to the acting performance of the call-girl and the grunts of the fighter, the scene was definitely like a drama. As the fighter pounded away at her insides, he was definitely giving it his all.

Malice waited until their sexual romp ended and allowed her to leave before fulfilling his sworn duty. His code was: never kill unnecessarily, and he recognized killing the call-girl would've been unnecessary. To him, she was at work so that made her an innocent bystander.

After the door closed behind her, he stepped out of the shadows of the room. The fighter jumped out of fright seeing the shadow standing in the bedroom doorway. He put on a pair of shorts. "What's good, son? I don't have any beef in the streets, so whoever you are, you got the wrong address."

Malice pulled out the sword, which was already stained with the souls of others he'd ridden the planet of. Seeing the glint of the steel, the man's face revealed his fear as he begin to panic. He moved around so quickly he bumped into the dresser causing it to shake.

Sensing he might try to escape, Malice ended any ideas he may have had and snatched his soul from him with a single downward slash technique, splitting his body open down the center. Malice was gone before his lifeless body fell back onto the bed.

**

Agent Saki Po roamed the streets of Chinatown. She figured, if anyone knew anything about the dismantling or mutilation of victims, it was her people.

It wasn't long before she worked up an appetite from all the walking, talking, and eavesdropping she'd done. Luckily, there was an egg roll shop was nearby.

She walked inside the restaurant and greeted everyone she passed with a bow. Sitting down on the cushion in the lotus position, one of the waitresses hurried over to her empty table. Noticing she was of Chinese descent, the waitress greeted her by speaking in their native tongue— Saki returned the honor by ordering in Chinese.

After taking her order, she hurried off to get it filled. Saki called out to her and told her to take her time since she wasn't pressed for time. She watched as an elderly

Asian couple interacted with one another at the table next to hers. It brought back memories of her mother and father, who'd died saving her life.

At the age of 14, she was performing at the International Martial Arts Committee in Beijing. It was her family's tradition because they were all highly skilled in the world of martial arts. Even at that age, Saki had already proven to be efficient in ten different styles of close quarters combat and efficient with the bow staff, projectiles, throwing weapons, and swordsmanship. Everyone who loved the arts had gone to watch her perform.

Her mother, father, and baby brother sat stage side. She performed with excellent proficiency. At the end, she bowed in all directions as the audience applauded with a standing ovation. It was a moment to remember.

However, after the show ended, disaster came to greet her and her family. Members of the Asian Triad approached her father outside of the arena. It was no secret that the majority of the Po Clan were assassins who worked for a criminal organization. And it definitely wasn't a secret that her mother and father were board members.

By the exchange of words, she could tell her father wasn't willing to agree to whatever terms the Triad had offered him. And it became more obvious when the ninjas stepped out of the darkness and surrounded them.

Her mother had positioned herself in front of her and her brother before unsheathing Twin Scorpion Short Swords and taking a defensive stance. Before the ninjas could engage, her father launched an attack of his own, killing three of the Asian Triad members. At the same time, her mother had taken down a couple ninjas of her own, clearing an escape route for their daughter and son.

"Run," her father shouted, "and keep running and never look back!" he told his children. He had wanted her mother to run with them, but she had refused to leave him to die alone. Saki's parents fought to their death, but they had hoped her and her little brother had gotten away and survived, and they had.

The waitress snapped her out of reminiscence when she sat the dishes onto the table and poured the hot tea. When she left again, Saki devoured the egg rolls smothered in soy sauce and the shark fin soup full of spices and herbs. As she sipped the tea, a Chinese lady who looked to be around her age and build walked up to her table. With a smile plastered on her face, the lady bowed and took a seat..

"My lady, I couldn't help noticing you from across the room. Is it possible that you're a friend, or someone I met long ago?" she asked in broken English.

Saki took another sip of the tea and sat the cup down on the table. "Possibilities are infinite." She stood and bowed.

"My name is Sia Po. Daughter of—

"Kechi and Dom Po. Yes, I know who you are cousin," Saki interjected.

"So, it really is you Saki?" Sia asked.

Saki nodded.

"After the death of your parents, the Po Clan disavowed their services to the Triad and went into secrecy. They still attempt to hunt us down, but their assassins never return to them. You get the picture," said Sia, discreetly.

Saki called the waitress back over to the table and ordered more food. She and her cousin sat, ate and talked about the past, and their present occupations. As fortune would have it, the restaurant belonged to Sia, and everyone who worked in it were members of the Po Clan.

"We haven't stopped our tradition of being the greatest of warriors. We have a training place setup in the basement," her cousin said proudly.

"That's honorable of you all to preserve our clan's culture. Anything I can do to help, I will," Saki replied sincerely.

Her cousin reached across the table and placed her left hand on top of hers. "Join us here, Saki. We live in peace for the most part. Like I said, every now and then assassins are sent our way, but to no avail."

Saki thought about it long and hard. She enjoyed her job at the bureau, but her loyalty belonged to her clan, and they were asking for her assistance. Between that and the fact she was being given the chance for revenge, her decision came easily.

"I'll turn in my resignation with the bureau in the morning," she said happily and without hesitation.

She rest her right hand on top of Sia's left, and Sia placed her right hand on top of hers. The two ladies smiled at one another.

Speaking in Chinese, Sia beckoned the restaurant workers to gather around the table. When she introduced them to Saki and informed them who her parents had been, they begin to kneel around her.

"Just as your mother and father led this clan, we pledge our loyalty to you, Saki Po, to lead the Po Clan according to the tradition established by our ancestors," Sia proclaimed.

As confirmation of her role as head, Saki accepted their pledge. She honored their request to abide with them for the remainder of the night. The following morning a couple of them would accompany her to the agency and hotel room to gather her personal belongings and give an official resignation.

CHAPTER SIX

Agents Amari Akoo and Trinity Taiga found themselves in a tight spot. Due to their African heritage, they found it difficult to blend in on the streets. Their difficulty was proven due to the fact of their current location and position. Inside a meat cooler in the back of a butcher's shop, Amari and Trinity hung upside down, stripped down to their undergarments. They did their best to disguise their fear by remaining silent and calm in the presence of their captors.

The men who had tied them up left the room. Trinity, who was upset at Amari for being so stupid by asking questions concerning the meat locker murders, tried to free herself from the bounds.

Amari, on the other hand, had succumbed to his fate. "Trinity, you're wasting your time," he said hopelessly.

She wiggled around enough until she gained momentum to sway from left-to-right. "Speak for yourself, Amari. I'm getting out of here alive. As a matter of fact, don't speak another word to me. If it wasn't for your stupidity, I wouldn't be hanging upside down like a pig ready to be slaughtered."

She was right, so he didn't say another word. He watched her change the direction of her motion from left-to-right to back and forward. After three attempts, she accomplished her goal of reaching her feet. Quickly and with true nimbleness, she untied her feet and flipped down, landing on her feet.

"Nice work, Trinity. Now, untie me so we can get the hell out of here," he said quietly.

Ignoring him, she took the plastic ties off her wrists and crept out of the cooler, leaving him behind— his expression was priceless. Out of all his years of working for the bureau, never once had he witnessed a fellow agent leave another agent to the wolves. But, here he was, and Trinity had done just that.

He closed his eyes, feeling as if he'd been dishonored. When he reopened them, standing before him were three women dressed in white butcher uniforms covered with plastic. All of three held hatchets. As they walked towards him, he closed his eyes again and welcomed each cutting edge.

They made a quick work out of the agent's body. After they'd bled him out like a pig, they untied his feet, letting his lifeless body fall to the plastic covered floor. Next, the proceeded to chop him up limb-by-limb and tossed his mutilated body parts inside a ten-gallon drum of acid. Afterwards, the three women rolled up the plastic, disposed the evidence, and mopped the floor clean.

***

The next morning, Agents Timothy Barnes, Peter Sanders, Dominique Townsend, Saki Po, Trinity Taiga and Tabitha Greene met with Director Wade Stevens in the conference room. Since Agents Butch Henderson, Hailey Timmons, Katherine Tolbert, and Amari Akoo weren't going to be attending, everyone presumed they were already dead.

Well, they knew Amari Akoo was dead because of the report Trinity had given the team concerning the previous night. Tabitha didn't give a report on her night out experience, instead, she sat back observing the body language of everyone else in the room.

"Well, it's obvious something big is going down around here. Four of Jersey's best agents are missing in action. More than likely, dead. It's hard to say since none of their bodies have popped up," the director said, before he turned his attention toward Saki and the two Chinese women who stood behind her. "Agent Saki Po, who are they and what are they doing here?"

"Director Wade Stevens, they are my family, and they've asked for my assistance. As of today, I'm resigning from the bureau indefinitely. It has been an honor serving a noble cause. Now, I must be of service to my family. Have a great, prosperous and long life." She replied without question.

Saki Po stood, and they left without saying another word.

Director Stevens looked around the table at the remaining five agents. "Anyone else planning an early retirement that I need to know about?"

"Maybe we're in over our heads on this one, Director Stevens," Trinity said as she relived her moment of captivity. *One second, Agent Akoo had been asking dangerous questions, and the next, they were surrounded by masked murderers.* "I mean, if you had seen how fast they were on Agent Akoo and I, you would realize and understand we're dealing with professional killers, real mercenaries. I say we call this one and take the advice of your conscience. You know . . . see the meat locker murders as karma."

"I guess that means you're out as well, Agent Taiga?" asked Wade.

She didn't respond verbally. Allowing her body to speak for her she slid back in the chair, got up, and made her exit. Now, they were down to four. Before he could respond, Tabitha jumped up out of her seat.

The director was flabbergasted. "Where are you headed, Agent Greene?"

"I'm about to go perform my morning ritual. I need to clear my head. I suggest the rest of you consider doing the same if you're planning on surviving," she answered.

She walked out and stopped at the receptionist's desk. Jennifer was on a call, but seeing her, she put the caller on hold. "What's up, babes?" she said, smiling from ear-to-ear.

"Agent Humphrey, we're on the job. We have to remain professional," Tabitha reminded her.

She gave her an 'I don't care' look, which made Tabitha laugh. "What do you want for lunch, Jenn?"

Jennifer smiled.

"Besides that, luv," Tabitha added, knowing what she was implying.

"There's a nice organic vegan spot around the corner. They've got some great meatless chicken," Jennifer said.

"Okay, luv. I'll see you at 12:30 for lunch," Tabitha told her. She tapped the top of the desk three times. It was a code they used at work to say I love you.

In response, Jennifer tapped it four, which was to say I love you more. It kept everyone out of their personal life.

Tabitha drove the Audi 8 over to the drama theatre. She got out and hurried inside, not wanting to miss the first act. She wasn't a minute late, nor was he. Right next to the seat she liked, sat Kenneth.

"Good morning, Ken. I see you enjoy invading my personal space," she said playfully.

"You know, Tab, try being a little considerate of another's personality, won't ya'. When I came out of the shower yesterday, I waited on you at the bar. It was kind of embarrassing having to find out from someone you had left," he said, reminding her of their last encounter.

"Aww. . . . That's so sweet of you," she responded.

"Go on with that sentimental jargon," he said, with a smirk on his face.

She pinched his left cheek and bumped shoulders with him. "Thanks for your concern."

Kenneth put his finger to his lips. "Shh . . . The act is about to start."

They sat in silence and watched the artists act out an Afrocentric version of Bonnie and Clyde. Without the sexual intimate portion, the play described the way he felt about her. It was pure brotherly love and it was obvious she'd accepted him to be just that. She draped her left arm around his shoulder, and they enjoyed the rest of the act.

When it was finally over they walked outside and stood in the sunlight next to her car and talked. Tabitha's watch alarm went off. She checked the time and it was 9 am sharp.

"Somewhere important to be?" Kenneth inquired.

She nodded. "As a matter of fact I do. In the ring kicking your ass again."

He burst into laughter. Being around her actually made him feel burden free. It was like all his demons fled from her presence. "Okay, round two it is."

They hopped in the car and drove to the gym. The owner and most of the fighters were glad to see them. Tabitha and Kenneth did a routine warmup exercise and stretch.

"Alright, Ken, today we turn it up a notch. Straight hand-to-hand close quarters combat," she said.

Ken chuckled while shaking his head. "I see now I'm going to have to show you what's really going on, Tab. Don't misquote me. You're good, but I'm out of your league."

"The ring is over there, Ken," she replied sarcastically, as she pointed with her index finger.

He could hear the irony in her voice. "Ooh . . . sounds like someone feels offended."

Her response was to walk down the aisles and get inside of the ring.

He shook his head, amazed by her self-confidence. She reminded him so much of his baby sister who had died at the hands of his mentor. Of course, he killed him once he gained the necessary skills of the ninja. After killing his master, he had taken over the guild.

Kenneth entered the ring with a serious expression etched across his face. Everyone gathered around ringside to watch the sparring match.

"We're about to see what's up with that big talk," she said, as she bounced around on her toes.

Kenneth suppressed his laughter. Keeping his straight face, he sat on his knees in the center of the ring and closed his eyes. "Give me your best shot, Tab."

She stopped bouncing around and stared at him. "Be serious, Ken."

"Oh, I am. If you can hit me once and knock me over, I'll buy you whatever you want," he said.

The chatter stopped. Kenneth's proposal had caught everyone's attention.

She nodded. "Alright, bro. I hope your checks don't bounce."

Tabitha walked up to him and tried to shoot him a thrust dragon knee to the chest. Without opening his hand Ken blocked and countered by shooting a straight and stiff closed fist blow right below her kneecap, causing her to stumble forward and into him. As her body made contact with his, he flipped her across his shoulder and onto her back, with an over the shoulder toss.

She bounced up off the mat and retreated to the far side of the ring. His eyes were still shut, and he let out an unbothered sigh. She decided to change her method of attack. Instead of coming straight forward, she circled around him as silently as she could.

Suddenly, she launched at him from the rear. Right before the initial contact of the judo chop she aimed at his upper right shoulder blade, he blocked with an upward brush block and shot her a left reverse elbow to the front of the thigh. She let out a painful grunt before finding herself going for another dive to the mat. He held on to her wrists and pulled her body forward while using his free hand to palm her abdominal area, forcing her off her feet and into the air over his back. With her body positioned before him on the mat, he applied pressure to the wrist he still held, causing her to tap the mat three times as hard as she could.

Being that Tabitha had tapped, Kenneth prostrated before opening his eyes and standing back to his feet. She remained lying on the mat in deep thought. For the first time in her life, she actually felt humiliated.

Ken took a deep breath and exhaled. "Tab, some people fight with their body, others fight with their mind, then there are us who fight with spirit. Knowing who and what you are aides you in deciding your true fighting style."

He helped her to her feet. This time when he came from the showers she was sitting at the bar snacking on a granola bar.

He sat down next to her. "What's going on inside of that mind, Tab?" he asked.

"Well, more than I would care to have there," she replied. She changed her sitting position in order to face him. "Where did you learn to fight like that?"

"That's a long story, Tab. Maybe when we both have free time again, I'll tell you rather than toss you around," he replied jokingly.

She looked at her watch. It was 11:45 am. "Yeah, I would like that. But speaking of time, is there anywhere special you would like to be dropped off? Because I have to meet my partner for lunch in a few minutes."

"No, I'm good. My place isn't too far from here," he said.

"Are you sure?" she asked.

He waved her off. "Go have lunch with your girlfriend, sis. I'm positive we'll see each other tomorrow. Maybe I'll even get to meet her, and we can all have lunch together."

She hugged him around the neck. "Bye Ken."

He hugged her back. "Aye. What I told you about the sentimental jargon?"

She smiled and turned to leave and couldn't help but to laugh out loud at his humor.

***

Mickey's phone rang. At the time, he was laid-back receiving some of the best oral pleasure he'd been given in a while, and needless to say, he wasn't up for talking. The only sounds coming from his mouth were the illegible moans and sighs of sexual gratification. He would've continued to ignore the irritable back-to-back ringing, but whoever the caller was kept calling without leaving a voicemail.

"Hold up. Let me answer this call," he said.

Katherine raised her head up from his lap and wiped her lips with the back of her hand.

He grabbed the cellphone off the dashboard and answered the incoming call. "Yo', what's good? And I do mean it better be good, my man. Matter of fact, it better be *damn good,* better than what was going down before you insisted on interrupting.

"Is that any way to treat a friend, Mick?" the female caller retorted. It was Valencia.

Realizing it was her, he signaled for Katherine to resume her position. She smiled and ducked her head back underneath the stirring wheel. Mickey combed through her hair with his fingers, enjoying the way her lips felt around him.

"What's going on, queen? What can I do for you?" Mickey asked.

"I was just checking in to see if you had any pertinent information for us," she replied.

"No, not at the moment," he said, with his eyes closed, still enjoying the fellatio Katherine was giving.

"Okay. Enjoy the head," she said and chuckled, 'cause you never know when it'll be the last time," and with that said, she ended the call.

Mickey tossed the cellphone back on the dashboard. Feeling the pressure rising, he reclined farther back in the driver's seat. "Climb on up here Kat. Let me have some of that good kitty."

She climbed on top of him and guided him inside of her. As she bucked on top of him wildly, he reached beneath her short skirt and gripped her buttocks. The two filled the air with sounds of pleasure until they reached the point of climax. Without saying a word, Katherine got out, hopped in her Mercedes, and drove off.

***

Trent called Dominique so they met up in a suite at his expense. They had come to the conclusion that sexing one another would be equally therapeutic session for both of them. She lay with her head propped against his shoulder. The secrecy was eating at her, and he could sense it.

"Luv, honesty is the best policy. Whatever is on your mind, let it go. Free yourself. Don't allow your thoughts to become cancerous," he said.

She sat up and looked him in the eyes. "You're absolutely right, Trent. I'm a federal agent. My name is Dominique—"

"Agent Dominique Townsend. You're originally from North Jersey. You have a daughter in the military. Need I continue?" Trent interrupted.

She looked at him, confused as to how he knew so much about her, when she knew nearly nothing about him. "Well, damn. So much for undercover."

"Yeah, about that. Dominique, let it go. Trust me. I can't protect you if you continue chasing shadows," he said in a demanding tone.

"Are you trying to scare me into quitting my job?" she asked.

"No. I'm trying to save your life, Dominique. You don't seem to recognize death when it's looking you right in the face. Sooner or later, the shadows you're chasing will start to hunt you, and that's the moment we'll have to go our separate ways," he said seriously.

She leaned over and kissed his lips. "Whose side are you on anyway?" she asked, tilting her head to the side.

At that point, Trent realized his attempt to save her was pointless. And since it was pointless, he changed the subject. After they talked for a while he got out of bed and got dress. "Come on."

She looked at the time and it was almost midnight. "Where are we going this time of the evening?"

"There goes the agent part of you rearing its ugly head," he said, shaking his head. "You'll see when we get there. Come on."

After they dressed, they took the Amtrak out to place they first met. She recognized the place immediately. "I remember this place."

"Yeah, I know. Let's go inside. I have some people who are dying to meet you," Trent told her.

They entered the club. It was Thursday so the place was almost empty. There were only two women sitting at the bar and both spoke to Trent as he walked by. The silence felt creepy to Dominique, and the chill she felt made it seem even creepier.

The two women who sat at the bar got up and followed them into the back hallway.

"Who's your friend, bro? Is she here for the main event or is she part of the main event?" one of the ladies said, eyeing Dominique curiously.

Trent's lack of a response told them all they needed to know. He stopped at the third door on the left and sighed before opening it because he knew death awaited Dominique on the other side.

"Do you have a special request, bro?" Valencia asked.

"As always, nice and slow. It reminds them of the things that matters," he said.

As he opened the door, Angel and Valencia put blades to Dominique's throat. She felt as if her legs were about to give. "What's going on, Trent? What have you done?"

"Shhh . . . Trent can't save you now," Angel said. Her face showed no remorse.

Trent held the door open as they escorted Dominique in at knifepoint. The room was full of unfamiliar faces with the exception of two— Agents Barnes and Sanders, who were naked and hogtied in the middle of the room.

Angel shoved Dominique in the back, causing her to stumble forward and fall beside her fellow agents.

"Timothy? Peter?" She looked from one to the other, as if they could help her. In her mind, she prayed it was all some kind of sick joke.

They were gagged, so their responses was nothing more than mere muffled sounds. Dominique looked around the room until she locked eyes with Trent. Everyone besides him held swords or daggers in their hands.

A few seconds later, a clean shaven, bald man entered the room.

"Whoa! Who and what do we have here?" the bald-headed man exclaimed enthusiastically.

"Federal agents. Supposed to be the best in the business," Valencia answered.

The statement caused him to smirk. A worthy challenge was the one thing he lived for, especially when it was for sport. And *this* was for sport. "Oh yeah? Someone cut them loose," he ordered.

Without hesitating, Angel cut the ropes. Timothy and Peter stood up which put Dominique between them. Seeing their loyalty to each other put a big smile on his face. "Trent, front and center."

Trent moved from his position, to stand in front of the three agents. They realized he was the only thing standing between them and the door.

"Here's the deal. You all have one chance. If you can make it pass my brother, you're free to go. No need to say what happens if you can't," the man said. He stepped out of the way and stood against the wall with the others. "By the way, you have seven minutes," he added.

Trent stared into Dominique's eyes as Timothy and Peter rushed him. He blocked every blow they attempted to hit him with without ever taking his eyes off her. After a minute of toying with them, he started breaking the two agents off. Timothy threw a right cross but he caught it in mid swing and broke his arm before catching him with a thrust kick to the gut, sending him face-first to the tiled floor.

Peter came at him with a grappling maneuver. Trent sent him to the floor after hitting him with a flurry of elbows. Still staring into Dominique's eyes, he stomped on the side of each man's knees, shattering bones, causing them to cry out in agony.

Trent took a step towards Dominique, but before he reached her, the clean-shaven man stopped him.

"Well done, brother. You may rest now. Her time will come momentarily. For now, she shall bear witness to the true face of death. Chop, chop," the man said.

It was a horrific scene. Dominique watched as they butchered Agent Barnes and Sanders. It was like watching hyenas on a fawn, and it was over in seconds.

"Angel, front and center," the man ordered again.

Everyone else returned to their places against the wall. Angel stood before Dominique with blood dripping from her Dragon Daggers.

"Agent Townsend, you already know the rules as well as what's at stake," he said, as he backed up against the wall.

As Angel sheathed the daggers, Dominique tried to catch her off guard with a sneak attack. She threw a nice three-jab combination that Angel weaved. She continued to move straight forward, and with her hands behind her back, Angel bobbed and weaved every punch.

"This is a waste of time," Angel said.

All of a sudden, moment, Dominique spun around with a 180 spinning back fist, which Angel sidestepped and caught her arm in a firm grip. With lightning speed, she used her free hand and unsheathed one of her daggers, stabbing Dominique in the bicep and neck before cutting her throat.

With all three agents dead, the main event was over. The mercenaries got rid of the corpses, cleaned up the evidence, and showered.

Willie Slaughter

CHAPTER SEVEN

The following morning, Tabitha and Jennifer sat in front of the computer in the minicomputer room at Jennifer's house. Jennifer tapped in a series of commands and clicked on several icons that popped up on the screen, before plugging the mini USB into the USB port of the cellphone.

"Okay, babes. Let's see what we got here," she said.

Although the cellular device looked simple, it proved to have a complicated encryption code that kept them out of the personal data bank of the phone.

"That was real smart of this guy, or whoever installed this cyber firewall. But not smart enough," she said, clicking on the crossing swords icon.

Before she could get into the program, she had to enter several passwords and answer many more security questions. As soon as she got clearance, she entered another series of commands and pressed enter.

"That should do the trick," Jennifer smiled and said, as she leaned back in the chair.

While the computer was loading, Tabitha got up from the chair she was sitting in and sat on Jennifer's lap with her body facing toward her. She kissed her on her soft lips and grind her hips against her lap.

She responded by exploring beneath her nightgown with her left hand and sliding two fingers inside of her.

Tabitha moaned passionately between kisses. She grinded slowly, but forcefully onto her fingers. Jennifer could feel the temperature within her sex rising around her fingers as she was nearing a release— a release that came smooth. She used her fingers to wiggle inside her embracing the flowing fluids around them.

"Tabby?" Jennifer moaned.

Tabitha kissed her desirously. "Yes, baby?"

"We're at work. Remember?" Jennifer reminded her.

"True, however, we're also at home. Meaning, business can be mixed with pleasure," Tabitha stated before she climbed off top, and sat back in the chair beside her.

The computer screen showed a big green check, confirming it had completed the loading commands.

"See, we're right on schedule. I know. You're welcome, Jenn," Tabitha said and giggled. Her sense of humor was one of a kind. "Now, let's crack this whip for real."

Jennifer cracked the joints of both hands before entering a search and retrieve all data command. Upon pressing enter, the information begun filling the screen at a rapid pace. They looked at the screen attentively. Whoever the guy had been in the alleyway was well connected and he'd made more money transactions than either of them cared to count.

"Hold up right there," Tabitha said.

Jennifer stopped the search engine when she saw Tabitha's picture appear. She opened the text message it was attached to which had come from a contact listed as Mick. The named sounded familiar to Tabitha.

"Jenn, hon, can you pull up this contact's actual cellphone number and personal info?" she asked.

"Anything for you, babes. Coming right up," Jennifer said, and typed in a 'search personal contacts' information command and pressed enter. When the name and picture appeared on the screen, Tabitha's heart skipped a beat. There he was, her Uncle James' best friend, Mickey Freeman.

Jennifer noticed her sudden mood change and asked, "Is everything alright, Tabby? Do you know this guy?"

"At least I thought I knew him. He was my Uncle James' friend. . . . he was supposed to have been anyway," Tabitha said sadly.

Jennifer remembered her sharing the death of her uncle with her when they'd first met. How could she forget? She'd held her while she cried afterwards. The facts on the screen angered her because it was damaging the emotions of the love of her life.

"I know you're thinking what I'm thinking, Tabby. We're about to get to the bottom of this right now. What was Uncle James' phone number and the actual date of his death?"

Tabitha gave her the information she asked for. After she typed in the commands to bypass privacy codes to gain access to Mickey's phone and its data log that couldn't be cleared, Jennifer typed in James' number and the dates Tabitha had just given her. And just as they thought, he'd called him on that day. Remembering the time she'd left and the time of death, according to the coroner's report, the call was made minutes before. And Tabitha nor Jennifer believed in coincidence.

"Now, whose number is that?" Jennifer said, pointing at the screen.

There was another number that Mickey had also contacted earlier that same morning. The interesting part was, the number had called his phone back just minutes after the murder of her uncle. Jennifer pulled up the number to see if it was listed under his contacts.

"Malice. Who in the hell calls themselves Malice?" she wondered aloud.

"Well Jenn, if I had to guess, my answer would be people who kill with malicious intent. I wonder if his or her phone is still in service," Tabitha asked.

"There's only one way to find out," Jennifer said, and quickly typed in a show of service command. On file, the cellphone was still in service and had a recent call list. It was under contract, therefore, there had to be a name.

Tabitha had an unnerving feeling about the whole ordeal. Something told her that whoever this mysterious Malice character turned out to be was probably the murderer of her uncle and many more innocent people.

Jennifer waited impatiently for the data analyzer to retrieve the content. After about ten minutes of waiting, the name Kenneth Freeman popped up under the number.

"Look at the time, babes, it's time for us to clock in. I'll just set this to print out all the data until the copier runs out of paper," Jennifer said, then set everything up to print.

Not long afterwards, the two women took a long *steamy* shower together, got dressed, and headed out to work.

Tabitha entered the conference room, looking to confirm her suspicions. And when the only person she saw was Director Stevens, she knew they would never see the other agents again.

"Have a seat Agent Greene," Wade said.

She sat in the chair near the door. She could tell his nerves were wrecked by the way he paced the floor and rubbed his head repeatedly.

"I'm pulling the plug on this operation," he told her.

"Not yet, Director Stevenson. I think I'm on to something major. If my hunch is correct, this thing ties into the death of my uncle," Tabitha said quickly.

He stopped pacing and took a seat. "I'm all ears," he said, eager to hear the details.

Tabitha decided to fill him in on some of the info that would give reason to keep the investigation going. On the other hand, she opted to keep certain specifics to herself. After relating her thoughts, he looked at her with a new profound respect.

"Agent Greene, I can see why you're still alive. You know how to withhold information until necessary," the director said.

"Director Stevenson, it's obvious there's a mole or *moles* inside this bureau. I'm not ruling out that one of them is one of the federal agents who was a part of this operation," she said confidently.

He perked up as he contemplated her last statement. Normally, he would be defensive about such an allegation concerning a fellow agent, but due to everything she'd shared with him, he'd encountered a new outlook on such things.

"Alright, Agent Greene, you're the last man standing. Be careful. You're dismissed," he said with finality.

"Thank you, sir." She got up and left.

She stopped by the receptionist's desk and did her usual three taps. Jennifer was handling an important call, but not so important that she couldn't respond by tapping the desk four times. She watched the sway of Tabitha's hips until she bent the corner and was no longer in sight.

Tabitha was already dressed for her morning gym routine with Kenneth, so she decided to jog over to the theatre just to get an early start, and to help ease the tension of her and Jenn's newfound revelation.

As she turned the corner at the end of the street, out of her peripheral, she could've sworn she seen Agent Katherine Tolbert sitting in a car she jogged past. Instead of stopping, she changed pace and turned around, jogging backwards to get another look to confirm what she knew to be true. And sure enough, it was her.

To play it off as if the backwards tread was part of her routine, she kept to the pace and checked behind her every now and then. She could see Katherine on the phone.

After she turned the corner and made sure she was out of sight, she turned around and picked up the pace. It was something fishy going on, but this wasn't the right time nor place to put herself out there as bait to figure it out.

At the entrance of the theatre, she slowed to a fast-paced walk. The theatre was packed since it was Friday and most of the drama fanatics were off work. She entered the stage playroom and took her seat next to Kenneth, who always seemed to be a step ahead of her. He noticed the sharpness in her breathing.

"Early morning jog?" he questioned.

"Yeah, something to that nature," Tabitha said, as she looked around to see if anyone was acting suspicious.

Again, Kenneth took notice of her unusual action, which caused him to survey the room himself. "Is everything alright, Tab? You're not acting like the Tab I'm used to."

"Let's enjoy the entertainment, Ken. We'll talk afterwards," she replied.

He didn't push the issue. They sat quietly as usual. All of sudden, he felt the presence of danger enter the room. He surveyed the room again, and saw a female sitting on the back row, to the far left, by herself.

"Excuse me for a minute, lil' sis. I need to take a quick bathroom break." He excused himself and walked up the aisles at a casual pace. When he got closer to the woman, he gestured for her to follow him out. Without question she stood up and walked out beside him.

They stopped off in a blind spot. "What're you here to do?" he asked the familiar woman.

She pulled out her phone and turned the screen around to show him the picture. But the picture wasn't what he cared about. It was the contact who had put the contract out. She tucked the phone back into her overcoat pocket.

"Now you know why I'm here Malice. If you will excuse me, I have a job to do."

He looked around to make sure no one was in sight. And, as soon as the woman brushed past him, without giving it a second thought, he snapped her neck like a twig. He caught her limp lifeless body and dragged it over to a corner and propped it up against the wall. He pulled out a small canister and sprayed the solution onto Katherine's neck and facial areas, everywhere his hands had touched.

After Kenneth removed all evidence of his involvement, he walked back into the room just in time to catch the beginning of the next act. With the same calmness he always displayed, he sat back down beside Tabitha. She didn't say anything, however, she did check the time.

Midway through the act, they heard a woman screaming. The majority of the people inside hurried out into the hall to see what had happened.

Tabitha and Kenneth followed suit, pushing their way to the front of the crowd. When they finally saw the woman's dead body, all Tabitha could do was shake her head out of confusion.

"Everyone stay back! Someone call the paramedics," Kenneth commanded.

Realizing Tabitha had gone into a state of shock, he grabbed her by the shoulders and shook her. She looked into his dark brown eyes for the first time, and what she saw was love and loyalty. Moreover, she could see the cruelty and death he'd tried so hard to conceal. "Tab, do you know this woman?"

She shook her head in the negative. "Not really. She was watching me from her car this morning. Part of the reason I was a little paranoid earlier. I guess I don't have to worry about being paranoid anymore." She lied with ease.

"Come on. Let's get out of here. No need to stick around and be witnesses to a murder crime scene," he said.

Acting as if he had the slightest idea of what happened, he grabbed her by the arm and led her outside into the cool morning air.

Taking in a deep breath, she found herself doubled over, vomiting. Kenneth held her to keep her from falling over. When the crowd began to get even bigger, he lifted her onto his shoulder and hurried down into the terminal.

On the Amtrak, they sat in the back by themselves. Tabitha stared peered out through the window at the passing pedestrians. Her thoughts were scattered into a million broken pieces, and her ability to put the puzzle together was fading. "So, what's your story?" she asked. Although she was more than shaken up, she knew she had to say something because she hadn't spoken a word since they'd boarded the train.

Kenneth sighed reluctantly. "Tab, you definitely have perfect timing." As put together as he'd everyone believe, he was still human. Until Tabitha he really hadn't allowed himself to be sociable. He was a businessman, a private man, a cold-blooded murderer.

He told her the story about his family history. . . . how they were wealthy, professional, charitable businesspeople. He missed that part of his life. That part of his life was the closet thing to normal because it included his mother, father, and sister— all dead, thanks to a guild of mercenaries.

Another wealthy family had been fixated on destroying his family. His father had gotten caught up in a love affair, and his mistress lived in the home of the mercenaries responsible for his death. Since his mistress knew his father wasn't going to leave his mother for her, she hired the deadliest assassins money could buy. To avenge her heart, she had his entire family killed.

His father nor mother were alien when it came to the arts, so the first group the guild had sent ended up dead. That's when the master himself, along with the elites of the guild had shown up dressed in ninja suits. They slaughtered his mother and father unmercifully right before he and his sister's eyes. Remembering what happened next brought tears to Kenneth's eyes.

"Master Trion called Khadiesha over to him. He looked me in the eyes and said that I would thank him for it later. And that's when he snapped my little sister's neck like a twig. Instead of leaving me or killing me, he took me in as one of his pupils, and trained me in the way of the ninja.

"I was only ten then. I trained harder than anyone in the guild because I was determined to have my revenge— a revenge I fulfilled on my seventeenth birthday. Since then, I just stick to the daily routine I was taught," he said.

She wiped the tears from his eyes. Now, without him even telling her, she was one hundred percent sure who the ninja had been the night in the alleyway. Nevertheless, that also made her realize the possibility of him being her uncle's killer. Even if only for the time being, she knew she had to suppress the thought until the puzzle was complete. As of now, he was proving himself to be a major piece.

***

Saki was down in the basement with the Po Clan. She stood in the center of the room while everyone else sat in lotus on the soft mats. Speaking in her native tongue, she called out to one of the young men in Chinese.

He jumped to his feet and joined her in the center.

They bowed to one another and proceeded by positioning themselves in their fighting stances. Just as they were preparing to start, she heard a faint sound coming from the stairwell. She put a finger to her lips and gestured everyone quiet. She circled around the young man with her back toward him, as she looked about the room awaiting the unknown.

As she stepped to his right side, the projectile cut through the stillness of the air. She caught it between her forefinger and middle finger. Looking in the mysterious direction it had come from, she spun 180 degrees and threw it back into the shadows. Everyone heard the loud *thumping* sound of a body hitting the floor.

"Fángshǒu zhènxíng!" Saki yelled, ordering everyone into 'defense formation' in Chinese.

By the time they'd gotten in position, three ninjas stepped out as if by magic. All three unsheathed their swords. Sia tossed Saki a sword and grabbed one for herself. They directed the rest of the clan to stay back.

The two cousins stepped between the middle of the three ninjas who had begun circling around them. Before they could make a move, the ninjas attacked, but their swords were met by pure swordsman skill. Saki and Sia had cut them down in no time.

Sheathing the swords, the two faced each other and bowed. Others hurried about to clean up the dead bodies.

Finally, I've tasted revenge, Saki thought to herself.

CHAPTER EIGHT

When Katherine didn't report back to him, Mickey had chalked it up to a failed attempt. After receiving the news of her death at the theatre, he knew it had to be true. He had to give it to Tabitha, she had all of her uncle's skills and none of his flaws. She kept her life in her own hands.

Tabitha Greene was the sole survivor of her bloodline and he felt as if he were destined to wipe them all off the planet. So, to him, it was imperative she die. It was obvious she was too much for the average assassin to handle alone, so he called the true masters of the trade.

Her phone rang twice before she picked up. "Mickey Mouse, what's on the agenda?" she answered.

He couldn't stand for her to call him that, but to get the job done, he would take all the verbal assault she dished out. "I heard about your head doctor's little mishap. Tragic," she said.

"Yeah. She served her purpose. But listen . . . about that. I'm sending you a photo of a mark. I want her dead before midnight," Mickey said.

He sent the picture of Tabitha to her phone, with a text that read $75,000. Valencia opened the text in her inbox. After reading the numbers, she downloaded the photo and set it as a screensaver.

"Who else have you sent this contract too?" she asked.

"They're dead Valencia. Now, are you up for the job, or should I call Malice?" he asked.

"No need to get all touchy, Mickey Mouse. It's an easy seventy-five. I'll even send you a finale picture if you would like," she replied smugly.

"Yeah, do that, Val," said Mickey and disconnected their lines. He stared at the picture of Tabitha. *Soon enough,* he thought to himself.

***

Valencia had return to the meeting. Malice was filling them in on the total amount of money they'd taken in since the week prior. It added up to sixteen million. Everyone was so excited they never questioned the absence of certain members of the guild.

"I can actually say, our success is granted to us because of our loyalty to one another, the blade and to death. If you have any loose ends to tie up, get it done before tomorrow. Tomorrow night we feast and allow our blades a moment to rest," Malice stated, commending the members of the guild.

"What's a moment?" she asked.

"For the sake of your blood thirst, Val, a week. We'll party and rest for a week," he reiterated.

"Fair enough. If that's the gist of this meeting, I swear to uphold the spoken law. Now if you'd all excuse me, I have some collards to clean and cook for dinner," she said.

The word collards caught his attention. He played it cool and kept his emotions under control.

"What, the Malicious Val has only one mark? What holiday is it?" Malice said teasingly.

Everyone laughed. They knew Valencia was known for taking out three to four targets in a day. Between her and Angel, six of the sixteen million had come from contracts they'd filled.

"Seventy-five and a worthy mark is enough to quench my thirst until further notice," she replied. Without saying more, she walked out with her gear in a duffle bag.

Of all the mercenaries in the guild, his uncle had to call Valencia, a true sister of the guild. One who Malice himself had respect for. Now, he was having mixed emotions.

He thought about calling his uncle to find out why he was hell-bent on having her killed, but he knew his uncle. To question his sinister mind was to add fuel to his diabolical thinking. His loyalty and love kept him at a stalemate. He didn't want Valencia to kill Tabitha, nor did he want to have to be the one to kill Valencia.

Trapped in his own silent inner-struggle, Malice grabbed his leather trench coat and left.

***

It was the weekend, so Jennifer and Tabitha slept a little later than usual. They lay naked on top of the covers holding each other. The alarm clock went off and Tabitha rolled over and pressed the snooze button.

"Rise and shine, sexy," she said to Jennifer.

Jennifer rolled over and put her head underneath the pillow. "Can't we just lay here for the day? You serve us breakfast in bed, I'll do lunch, and we do dinner together. Doesn't that sound great, babes?"

Tabitha got up and stretched on her tiptoes. Jennifer enjoyed the sight from behind, so much, she began rubbing on herself. Between her thoughts and the view, she didn't know which had made her cum so fast and hard.

"Sounds tempting, Jenn, but I'm not one to lay around all day. Besides fieldwork, I have the weekend preplanned and prepaid for us," she said.

Jennifer sat up in the bed. She liked the idea of them having outings together. "Okay, Tabby, you win. What's first on our agenda?"

"Naked yoga, lovemaking in the Jacuzzi, and a shower to start the events off right," Tabitha replied.

"I love your spontaneous ways, Tabby," Jennifer said smiling.

"That comes with loving me, Jenn," she responded.

And as they stared their day, they did everything in that order. Dressed in matching red Tommy Hilfiger body dresses, they took the Porsche out. Tabitha did the driving since she had done all the planning and knew where they were going. *Dangerously In Love* played on the radio. Jennifer turned the volume up a notch. "Due to everything that's happened, I'm nominating this to be our song."

"Don't you have a sense of humor, Jenn? I'm feeling it though," Tabitha said.

She pulled into the drama theatre's parking lot and parked. Tabitha looked in her purse to make sure she had the two tickets. Seeing them, she sighed. *Thank goodness I didn't lose them,* she thought silently, and grabbed them.

"Okay, sweetie, let's go. We have exactly twelve minutes before the show starts. That gives us five minutes to get settled, and seven minutes to get all the talking out of your system. Cool?"

"Cool, babes," Jennifer replied with a smile.

They walked in and she gave the doorman the two tickets. Tabitha grabbed Jennifer by the hand and led the way through the crowd, into the auditorium, and down the aisle to their stage side seats.

Already seated in the seat left of hers was Kenneth.

"Well, I would call this a pleasant surprise, but our commons are our commons. It's great seeing you, Ken," Tabitha said, as she took the seat next to him.

"Same here, Tab. Aren't you going to introduce me to your girlfriend?" Ken asked.

Tabitha blushed. "Oh. Yeah. Jenn, this is my friend slash brother Kenneth. Kenneth, this is my wife, Jennifer."

"How are you, Jennifer? Nice to finally meet you," he said sincerely.

"I'm okay, Kenneth. You can call me Jenn," Jennifer replied.

"And you can call me Ken," he responded.

It was six minutes until the show started. For a moment, seeing Tabitha so happy and relaxed, he'd forgotten the real reason for his being there. Back on track, he turned in the seat to face her.

"Listen, Tab, right now, you're endangering the life of your friend by having her seen with you in public. Not to mention, your own."

She looked confused. "What are you not telling me, Ken?"

"Forget about what you think I'm *not* telling you. Right now, I'm telling you, you and your friend's life are in danger. One of the most skilled mercenaries I know is coming for you," he said.

Tabitha looked over at Jennifer who wasn't paying them any mind. She could tell it was her first time at a live drama play because she hadn't blinked once. She turned her gaze back to him.

"What am I supposed to do, Ken?"

"Either she leaves here alone, or you. You don't need to be seen together."

Tabitha looked around, paranoid. "You mean, like, right now?"

"Yes, Tabitha, before it's too late," he demanded.

She didn't know if the rage rising inside was because of the idea of an assassin being after her or having to put an end to a greatly planned weekend. She decided to leave and let Jennifer enjoy the show. She told her something had come up, and it demanded her immediate attention, and that she was sorry for ruining the weekend.

"It's cool, Tabby. I know you'll make up for it. Or . . . we'll have Brother Ken here to foot the bill since he was the messenger of bad timing," Jennifer said.

They laughed.

"I see Tab found someone with an equal sarcastic sense of humor. It's very admirable. I'm sorry for the interruption, Jenn. And I will foot the bill no matter the ticket," he said reassuringly.

She leaned forward in the seat to look at him. "Sounds like a family trip to the Bahamas," she teased.

"If that's what you want. Look, the show is about to begin. Just tell Tabitha what it is you decide on, and I'll oblige," he replied.

Tabitha handed her the car keys and kissed her on the cheek. "See you when I get home, babes. I love you."

"I love you more, Tabby. Keep my wife safe, Ken. I'm counting on you," Jennifer said.

He had no greater intention. He simply nodded, and they left.

***

Valencia sat outside the motel watching the people go in and out. After a half hour of waiting on her mark to show herself, she grew a little annoyed. She walked into the lobby, and putting on her best smile, approached the front desk. "Hi. I'm looking for a friend of mines. Her name is Tabitha Greene. I believe she's staying in one of your best suites."

The guy at the desk flipped through the check in logbook until he came to her name. "Yes, a Tabitha Greene was staying in suite room 325. Unfortunately, she's no longer with us. She checked out almost a week ago."

Valencia suppressed her anger. She didn't like the idea of chasing ghosts. "That sucks. I haven't seen my friend since she came in the city. Do you know where I might be able to find her?"

"Miss Greene is a big drama fan, and I hear they got a great show going on over at the drama theatre today. If you want to start looking for her, I say that's your best bet," he replied.

"Thank you, sir," Valencia said.

"No problem. Glad I could help."

Valencia walked back out into the flow of pedestrian traffic. She entered the alley where she'd parked her forest green Kawasaki Ninja. After putting on the helmet and letting down the visor, she sped off. She reached the theatre just in time to see her mark walking down the sidewalk, heading for a terminal.

She rode on by and circled around back. Knowing where Tabitha was headed, she parked and started walking up the sidewalk opposite of her. She'd put on her biker shades and let her hair cascade around her shoulders for blending in purposes. When the mark turned to ride the escalator down into the terminal, she crossed over.

Valencia waited a couple minutes before riding the escalator down. She knew the Amtrak schedule, and it would be ten minutes before it reached the terminal where they were. Upon reaching the bottom, she saw Tabitha sitting on a bench, waiting calmly. To her, the calmness meant she was either confident in her abilities to defend herself, or her instincts of danger weren't up to par.

Fate had to be on Valencia's side. Reason being, the terminal was like a ghost town. She sat down on the bench beside her. Her closeness irritated Tabitha, so she put a little space between them by sliding over.

"It's such a beautiful day outside. It's a shame nobody's out and about," Valencia said, making small talk.

"Yes, it is," Tabitha replied.

"So, what's a pretty young thing like you doing all by yourself?" Valencia asked.

"For the record, I'm not single. I do swing that way, but I'm happy with who I'm with. Understood?" Tabitha replied.

Valencia allowed herself a moment of genuine laughter. She had to give it to her, she had the feistiness of a true fighter, which made the little conversation that much more entertaining.

"What the hell? You're Tabitha Greene right?" asked Valencia.

"It seems I've become very popular these days," Tabitha said, in a serious but sarcastic tone of voice.

"More like very dead," Valencia said and drew one of the Dragon Daggers. As she went for the kill, Tabitha, quick in reaction time, blocked with an inside sweeping hand while jumping to her feet. She took a defensive stance. "I was wondering when this part would come. Let's get it over with." She looked Valencia directly in the eye and didn't flinch.

Instead of drawing her other dagger, Valencia sheathed the one she had drawn. "Finally, a worthy challenge. I can actually say I'm working for my money today."

The two women went at it.

Kenneth had entered the terminal from the other end. He crept up slowly, watching the fight scene unfold. Tabitha was holding her ground but he knew it was only because Valencia enjoyed toying with marks she saw as a test to her martial combat skills.

Tabitha sidestepped the spinning back fist she threw, but her opponent was too quick and fluent with her motion for her to grab hold of her arm. She realized, the only way she would strike the highly trained assassin was to fight close quartered. So, as the killer kept up the frontal assault, she used a fluid-like Tai Chi blocking style to slide inside. Once inside, she served her a combination of elbows and knees that stunned her.

Tabitha swept her off her feet with a front leg sweep. She tried to follow up with a knee, but Valencia rolled out of the way and regained her footing. She spit blood from her mouth. "Alright, youngster. Playtime is over." Valencia closed her eyes and focused her energy inwardly.

Tabitha maintained a defensive stance while she moved in to attack. She attempted a roundhouse kick, but with her eyes closed Valencia, caught her right leg and slung her to the ground.

She was slow getting up. Kenneth could tell she was in pain from Valencia's counterattack, and in no shape to continue. But he knew she wouldn't give up, which put him in a difficult situation. He watched as she tried to attack Valencia again and again. Every time, finding herself in more pain.

Valencia opened her eyes and drew her daggers. "Thanks for the challenge, Tabitha. It's been real."

Tabitha was too tired and injured to do anything other than stand. Valencia rushed in for the kill but found herself tumbling to the concrete and hitting the wall. Kenneth had intervened before he knew it.

"Tabitha, run! Get out of here!" Malice screamed.

"But the Amtrak will be here soon," she replied weakly.

Malice shook his head, knowing the train wasn't coming. "No, it won't Tabitha. We control the city's transportation as well as other things. Now go while you still have a chance."

She began limping towards the escalator. Valencia had shook off the trauma caused by the surprise attack. She saw her mark making a run for it and went after her, but Kenneth stood in her way.

"What are you doing brother? She's my mark," Valencia said.

"Just let her go, Val. I'll give you whatever you've been promised by contract. Just let her be," Malice pleaded.

Valencia wiped the blood from the corner of her lip. Malice, she drew my blood. I can't let her get away with that. Maybe if you would've shown up before time, I would've agreed to your terms."

Although she was halfway up the escalator, Tabitha had heard their exchange of words clearly. It was no longer a mystery who he was. Tears from heartache flowed from her eyes.

"Don't make me do this, Val," he pleaded.

She looked up toward the escalator. When she was no longer able to see Tabitha she became angry. "Malice, tell me, have you chosen an outsider over our family? Will you kill me for her?"

He didn't respond.

To her, his silence said all that he couldn't. She laughed hysterically. "I wonder what your uncle would think of you. He's the one who sent out the contract."

"I tell you what Valencia," he said, as he took off his leather trench coat and sat it on the bench. "If you can make it pass me, she's all yours." He looked at the time on the Presidential Rolex he was sporting. "It's 11:29 am. The Amtrak will be coming at 11:40. That gives you eleven minutes."

"I'll only take six." She launched at him with a whirlwind attack. He suffered a flesh wound on his right forearm from one of the Dragon Daggers. She stared into his eyes as she licked his blood off the blade. "Sweet."

She went in with another full throttle attack. She was using a unique style of slash and thrust cloak and dagger along with jujitsu styled kicks. Malice stayed on the defense. He blocked and countered with open palm strikes.

"Valencia, I don't want to kill you," he said.

"Too late. You killed me when you chose her. I'm supposed to be your sister." She swung wide, hoping to catch him off guard, but didn't. He caught her with a thrust kick to the gut causing her to double over forward. Out of instinct, he took her down with a dragon knee to the face. For the first time, she'd dropped her daggers.

He stood, towering over her, hoping she would stay down and give up on killing Tabitha, but it wasn't happening. Valencia sprang back to her feet. She closed her eyes to gain the focus along with the strength she needed. Malice sighed heavenward, knowing his choices had diminished.

He closed his eyes and reset his energies within. He reveled in the burning sensation of the energy traveling the full length of his body. He could feel her heartbeat, and knew she was coming straight at him. He sensed that her energy was just as conflicted as his, if not more.

Valencia flipped over his shoulder. As she landed to strike, Malice grabbed her by the throat and squeezed until he crushed her windpipe. Although he wanted to cry, he knew it wasn't the time or place. Quickly, he gathered her daggers and his trench coat.

He placed the daggers back inside the sheathes and wrapped his trench coat around her body. The Amtrak came. The passengers were in such a hurry they paid them no mind. He picked her up and carried her onto the train. And as the train pulled off, he stopped fighting back his tears.

Willie Slaughter

CHAPTER NINE

It was only twelve noon, so Tabitha knew Jennifer would still be at the drama theatre. She limped through the parking lot over to the Porsche and got in the passenger's seat. She reclined the seat so she wouldn't be visible. Her body was in so much pain, she fell asleep.

***

Saki was out and about, doing some herbal shopping for her family's restaurant, when she saw Jennifer exit the drama theatre. Having not seen her in a while, she decided to pull into the parking lot and have a little chat, to see how she'd been doing. Jennifer almost didn't recognize her dressed in her traditional clothing.

"Saki! How have you been?" Jennifer said happily.

The two women hugged.

"Great actually. I saw you coming out of the theatre and wanted to say hello since it's been a while. I didn't know you liked drama," Saki said.

Jennifer shook her head, smiling. "Me either until today. Tabitha bought us tickets."

"Where is Tabitha?" Saki asked.

Jennifer shrugged her shoulders. "She was called to duty right before the show started. But she's alright."

"Let me walk you to your car to give us a few minutes to catch up," Saki said.

"Of course," Jennifer replied.

The two ladies scrolled through the parking lot, engaged in friendly conversation. With the Porsche in sight, Jennifer noticed something looked out of place. Saki noticed the suspicious look on her face.

"Is something wrong?" she asked in a concerned tone.

"Yes. I didn't let the passenger seat back before we went inside the theatre," Jennifer answered.

"Stay behind me," Saki said, approaching the car with caution. When she looked inside, panic shot through her being. She walked back over to where she'd left Jennifer standing and handed her the keys to her car.

Jennifer took the keys. "What are these for?"

"They're the keys to my car. Don't ask any questions at this time. Just hand me your car keys and follow me. You have to trust me, Jennifer," Saki said.

Jennifer complied without an argument. Saki hopped in the Porsche and eased the door shut. The sight of Tabitha's battered, and bruised body was disturbing. When Jennifer pulled up beside her in her Mitsubishi Eclipse, she put the car in drive and led the way.

Tabitha came back to consciousness when she pulled behind the restaurant. Her vision was kind of hazy so she still couldn't make out where she was. Saki had gone inside and come back out, followed by three of the Po Clan's members who helped get Tabitha inside. Jennifer followed them in tears.

"She's going to be okay, Jenn. You go take the groceries upstairs and stay there. My cousins will see to it that you're provided for. I'll stay down here and see to Tabitha's fast recovery. Okay?" Saki said.

"Okay," Jennifer replied. She grabbed the bags and walked up the stairwell, leading into the main body of the restaurant.

When she was gone, Saki began giving orders in Chinese to those assisting her. They stripped Tabitha naked and washed her body.

One of them came back with a China cup and handed it to Saki. "You must drink this, Tabitha. It will ease the pain."

She nodded. Saki held her head up while she poured the hot fluid inside her mouth. Tabitha grimaced from the sour taste.

"Although it's not tasty, it's guaranteed to make you feel one hundred percent better. Unfortunately, you'll be sleeping for the remainder of this day and most of tomorrow," Saki assured her.

As she faded away from consciousness, her last word was *Malice*. Saki gave further instructions in Chinese. Two of the young men left out and came back carrying a bathtub that they sat next to the table Tabitha lay unconscious on.

The others began breaking up herbs and tossing them inside the tub. One poured steaming water and another stirred the mixture with a giant paddle.

Once they were satisfied with the healing concoction, four of them picked her body up off the table and laid her in the tub.

***

Mickey was lounging, enjoying the taste of a Garcia Vega when the doorbell rang. Not too many people knew where he lived or came to his house, so it had to be someone important. He got up from the recliner and made his way to the front door. He peeped out the peephole. Realizing it was his nephew, he opened the door.

"Nephew, what's going on? Come in," he greeted.

Malice picked Valencia's corpse up and walked in carrying her in his arms. Mickey closed the door behind him and locked it. He hurried down the hall behind Malice.

"Is that who I think it is?" he asked knowingly.

Still no response. He kept walking until he reached the door leading to the attic. His uncle opened the door.

"What happened, Malice?" Mickey asked, his tone laced with panic.

The memory alone brought tears back. He walked up the stairs carrying her body lugubriously. A chill crept up his spine because of Malice's silence. He didn't know whether to keep pestering him until he answered or turn around and run like hell.

In the attic, he laid her body on the floor. He unwrapped the trench coat from around her body, placed her daggers in her hands, and folded her arms across her chest. His uncle watched silently while he mourned.

"Listen, Kenneth, whoever did it will pay with their soul. Blood-for-blood. I promise you," his uncle said.

The rage rising inside had reached its boiling point. Malice stood to his feet, and before Mickey knew it,

Malice had him pent against the wall. The look in his eyes was the epitome of his name.

"You're in no position to ask any questions, Uncle. I'll ask the questions, and if I think you're lying, I won't hesitate to rip you apart limb-by-limb. Do you understand me?" he said demandingly.

"Yes, I understand. We're family. I have nothing to hide," Mickey responded.

"Tabitha Greene, who is she? And why are you so bent on seeing her dead?" Malice asked.

Mickey laughed nervously. "So, you'll kill the uncle, but protect the niece?"

Malice slung him to the floor. He was confused and Mickey knew it.

"Yeah, the mark in Patterson, New Jersey. His name was James Greene. He was the guardian of his niece Tabitha Greene, daughter of Terrance and Martha Greene. Everyone believed their deaths had been accidental, but they were far from it. Those thugs were paid a handsome amount to pull the job off," Mickey said.

Malice frowned. "When you say Martha, are you referring to Martha Greene whose maiden name was Martha Freeman?" He walked over to Mickey and snatched him up. "Are you talking about my Aunt Martha?"

"I can explain if you'll allow me to, Kenneth," he replied.

He let go of Mickey. "I'm listening," he said through clenched teeth, "now explain."

Mickey smoothed his shirt over. "The Greene Family was, and still are, just as wealthy and dangerous as our family. At our arrival to the United States from the Virgin Islands, our families made a pact. We wouldn't marry into each other's family. However, we would be strictly business partners. Your grandfather, grandmother, and her grandparents all signed the contract with the blood of the wicked, so to speak.

"Together our families built empires off of the blades of their swords. Everything was going great until Terrance and Martha met at an annual function, celebrating the families' success. I foresaw the breech of the contract and tried talking to both, Terrance and Martha, but they refused to follow our families tradition, and followed their hearts.

"They married, and Martha gave birth to Tabitha. Honestly, I wanted to kill them before all of that transpired, but my mother wouldn't allow it. Hell, even my father was against me doing it. So, I devised a plan and paid a small fortune to see to it being done.

"They were supposed to have killed the girl too, but by her being so small, they missed the most important mark. The sole heir to both the Greene and Freeman Estates, and all assets. A mistake that bit them in the ass, because she trained and revenged their deaths by slaughtering both gangs singlehandedly," Mickey explained his recollection.

Malice nodded. "I recall reading about those stories in the newspapers."

"Of course, we all did. So, to answer your questions, Tabitha Greene is my niece and your first cousin. And I want her dead to end the whole Greene bloodline. I'll see to it she pays with her life for killing Valencia," Mickey said.

Malice burst out in uncontrollable laughter for several reasons. One, his uncle for believing Tabitha could've killed Valencia, and two, a blood feud that only his uncle had been concerned with.

Mickey frowned. "What? You think I made this story up?"

Malice shook his head and continued to laugh. "I'll give it to Tabitha, she's a great fighter, but she's no match for a ninja. I was there, Uncle. Without using the dark arts, Valencia would've been beaten. Matter of fact, she was getting hammered pretty bad. But, when she was tired of toying with Tabitha, the tides changed."

"Well, who killed Valencia?" asked Mickey.

"I did. And now that I know Tabitha's my blood, I don't feel as bad. I knew it was something special about her when we met on the Amtrak after I killed her uncle," Malice replied. Now that he knew who it was, he felt remorseful for murdering the last of her blood on the Greene side.

Mickey had a look of pure hatred on his face. "You betrayed your own code? You dishonored me?" He rushed towards his nephew swinging wildly.

Malice ducked the punches before tucking and rolling over to Valencia's corpse. When Mickey tried to advance him again, he unsheathed the Dragon Daggers that were in Valencia's hands, and went to work. In memory of her, he used her favorite whirlwind attack. He cut him a thousand times on different areas of his body before slitting his throat. He returned the daggers to their rightful owner with an apology. It was never his M.O. to be sloppy or leave any evidence behind, although his attitude was carefree at the moment. He went downstairs and found what he needed to do the job.

He dossed the ether around the attic and on the bodies, and made a trail leading to the kitchen. He lit a match and tossed it onto the trail of ether, and watched it burn until it reached the stairwell of the attic. Knowing it would continue burning, he walked out the back door and set out at a nice jogger's pace around the block.

CHAPTER TEN

Morning came quicker than Malice cared for it to. Instead of going home, he'd slept at the guild's slaughterhouse. It was the one place he knew he could go and collect his thoughts without distractions. Although he hadn't opened his eyelids, he felt their presence around him.

He knew Angel and Trent were standing in the room watching him. He sat up on the couch before opening his eyes. The two loyal assassins bowed, and he bowed back.

"Angel? Trent? How are you?" he said.

"There's been a tragedy, brother. Your uncle and Val's bodies were found burnt to a crisp inside of Mickey's house yesterday around five in the evening. Our condolences for your losses, moreover, we mourn the loss of our sister Valencia," Trent informed him.

Malice lowered his gaze as the memory replayed repeatedly in his mind. The death of his Uncle Mickey didn't bother him however, the deaths of James and Valencia did.

They sensed he was deeply troubled by the news. Angel sat next to him and held him close.

"We all mourn for you because of the burdens you bear, brother. Maybe we should have never ceased in training hard. Since we stopped, several of our brothers and sisters haven't returned. So, I vote that we revert back to the ways of old," Angel said.

"I second the vote, brother," Trent agreed.

Malice nodded to show he was in agreement. He stood up and stretched. He thought about the story Mickey had told him.

"Since you two are elders, see to it that the training is done." "Excuse me, I have some people to go meet." He grabbed his coat and walked out the door.

***

Tabitha had awakened from her rest. The first person's whose face came into view belonged to Jennifer. She had dark lines around her eyes from the lack of sleep. Saki came into view, smiling down at her.

"And she lives. Let's get her up," Saki said.

They helped Tabitha out of the tub of herbs.

Jennifer gasped at the sight of her body. The bruises and cuts were gone. Sia found her expression amusing. "Jennifer, there's no greater cure than those produced by nature and used naturally. And a little faith in the natural helps with the healing process."

Jennifer hugged Sia and Saki. "Thank you so much. I don't know how I'll ever repay you, but I will."

Saki said something in Chinese. One of the women ran out of the room and returned carrying some clothes for Tabitha. She assisted her with dressing as well.

"Nonsense, Jennifer. You owe us nothing but loyalty and respect. Tabitha, on the other hand, owes me some herbs and an explanation. So, if everyone would, please leave us to discuss a matter in private? Not you Saki. You stay." Sia said.

Everyone, besides Saki, Sia and Tabitha walked up the stairs. Sia shut and locked the basement door before speaking. "Before you slipped from consciousness yesterday, you said something that caught my attention. You spoke the word *malice*. Now, were you referring to a person or an act? Because, depending on your answer to this question, you're in over your head."

"Malice is a person I know. He's like my brother," Tabitha replied.

A look of surprise crept across Sia's face. "So, you're saying you managed to befriend the greatest assassin in America? Do you know the way of the ninja, Tabitha?"

"To answer your first question, yes, it seemed to happened that way. And, no, I haven't a clue. He tried explaining it to me, and he showed me a thing or two while humiliating me in a sparring match. But Val, I believe he called her, did all the damage that you healed away from my body," Tabitha said, reliving the horror.

Sia frowned. What Tabitha was saying wasn't adding up. "So, how did you manage to escape death? The Malicious Val never misses her mark."

Tabitha looked at Saki who responded to Sia's pleading eyes by hunching her shoulders. "Malice intervened. If you don't mind me asking. How is it you know so much about these people?" she asked.

Sia sighed. "The old master of the guild. Your friend is now the master of Trion Li Xan. A master of the dark arts that makes up what you call ninja. He was the one the Triad sent to manage their affairs to find and murder any of our clan."

"The same master that Malice killed?" Tabitha asked, remembering what Malice had told her.

Sia nodded. "So, the great ninja has confided in you. Obviously, he feels something special about you."

"Can't be too special, since it was him who murdered my Uncle James," Tabitha shot back.

"Did this happen before or after you met him?" asked Sia.

"Before. But what difference does it make?" Tabitha replied.

Sia sighed. "Young lady, if he'd known James to be your uncle, he would still be alive. And whoever sent the contract would've died in his place. That's the way of the ninja. They're hearts are as ruthless as the blades they wield."

Tabitha stood up and stretched. She felt rejuvenated. "Do me a favor. Keep Jenn here until I return."

"Where are you going?" Sia asked out of concern.

"If I tell you, you might have me followed, and I don't want to endanger anyone else's life," she answered.

"Tabitha, we could follow you into the shower without you knowing. I only asked to make sure you knew the path you are about to travel," Sia said.

"I hope so. Can I borrow your car, Saki?" Tabitha asked.

Saki gave her the keys.

"Thanks. Sia, by any chance do you know where this guild is located?" Tabitha quizzed. Sia gave her the address and she typed it into the GPS on her cellphone.

"Thanks again. I'll see you later on this evening," she said, as she left through the rear exit.

She hopped in Saki's Eclipse and drove off.

***

Malice stood outside in front of the Freeman's Estate. He was having conflicting thoughts about going inside, but he had a lot of unanswered questions he would demand to be answered. He hated feeling as if he'd been used. And with that thought in mind, he walked up to the front door and knocked using the brass knocker.

One of the maids opened the door with a smile that quickly turned into a curious frown. It was like she was trying to put a name to his presence. She looked him over a couple times. "I know you're a Freeman. I just can't figure out whose boy you are. I reckon it's old age catching up with me."

"Mrs. Ethel, it's me, Kenneth," he said.

She looked at him closely. "Good Lord! Boy, you've grown! Just look atcha! A handsome and strong man!"

He laughed. "Thanks for the compliment. Listen, I come to see my grandfather and grandmother."

"Come on in, baby. They'll be glad to see you," she said.

He followed her through the place. Although he hadn't been there in years, his memories of roaming the hallways were fresh. They came to a stop before the double doors which opened up to a mini bar room.

"Hold up right here while I announce your presence," she said, and stepped inside the room. About three minutes later, she returned. "They'll see you now. I'm about to go and personally bake your favorite fig cake. Don't sneak off without eating it either."

"I won't, Mrs. Ethel," Malice promised.

He sighed and walked through the doors. His grandfather and grandmother were enjoying their morning tea. Seeing him, they sat the cups down and greeted him with hugs. As they settled back in their recliners, his grandfather motioned for him to sit as well.

"The ghost of this family has materialized. Is something wrong, Kenny?" his grandfather questioned him.

"Pops, Mickey is dead," Malice stated firmly.

His grandfather looked at him nonchalantly. "And you probably killed him. So what? After the trouble he caused this family, that's music to a sore set of ears." He looked at the troubling expression written all over his grandson's face and knew there was more. "What's really got you bent all out of shape, son?"

"What's the big deal with our family and the Greene's?" Malice asked.

The old man sat up straight. The look on his face wasn't one of hatred, but more so surprise. "What Greene have you met?"

"Thanks to your son, Mickey, I met James. He's no longer with us either," Malice replied.

His grandfather frowned. "Why not? What the hell happened? James Greene was a great man, and the last of the true Greene blood."

Malice shook his head, remembering the incident. "Tragic. However, you're wrong. He's not the last. Aunty Martha and Uncle Terrance have a daughter. Her name is Tabitha Greene."

His grandmother almost dropped her tea. "What did you say the child's name is?"

"Tabitha Greene, Grandma. Why?" he asked.

"Tabitha was my mother's name. Boy, she loved Martha," his grandma said.

"Terrance and Martha's deaths wasn't by accident like you think. Before I killed Mickey, he told me the whole story about how he paid the gangs to stage the shootout in order to kill them because neither of you would consent to their deaths over the broken pact. But Martha and Terrance weren't his main targets. He wanted their child dead more than anything," Malice explained.

His grandfather stroked his chin, deep in thought. His son's treachery had caught up with him and justice had been served. "So, the slime ball thought by having them and their daughter murdered he would become the heir of everything. But he had to know that you would have to be killed too. Because the birthright of your father passed down to you. You did a fine job killing that snake."

Tired of talking about it, his grandmother changed the subject. They sat and discussed the weather, nice vacation resorts, and future investments. The maid had brought them lunch, which came with the fig cake as a dessert. They ate and continued to talk.

"So, what are we going to do?" Malice asked.

His grandmother frowned. "Kenny, you need to come back home. You've loss some marbles. What are we going to do? You're going to go find our granddaughter and bring her to her blood."

She got up and walked out of the room, mumbling. His grandfather held his hand up to stop him. It was obvious he didn't know the old lady too well.

"Kenny, words from the wise. I suggest you be on your way, and don't show your face around here again unless Tabitha's with you," his grandfather warned.

"She's upset?" Malice asked.

His grandfather nodded. "Yes, she is. And she's going to remain upset until her granddaughter is standing before her. In other words, for the sake of my ears and your life, make it happen in twenty-four hours captain."

"I'll see to it," Malice said.

His grandfather walked over to a big bookcase. He searched until he found what he was looking for. He pulled the picture album from its place and sat it on the table. "I want you to take this picture book with you."

He flipped through the book, showing Kenneth all the pictures of Martha and Terrance together before, on, and after their wedding. He also showed him pictures of the two families standing together. Looking at the pictures brought a different emotion to the surface of the old man he'd never seen.

His grandfather exhaled deeply. "Man, those were the good ole days. Anyway, take this book with you. Maybe it'll balance things back out. Now, go make your grandma happy."

Kenneth grabbed the book and left.

***

Tabitha walked into the slaughterhouse determined to speak to Kenneth. Inside, she stepped to the first person she saw wearing a butcher's uniform. "Excuse me, ma'am. I'm here to see a friend of mines."

"I doubt that very seriously. I've never seen you around here before now. Anyway, who's this friend you think you have here?" Angel said.

"His name is Ken. Well, his name is Kenneth, but I call him Ken," Tabitha replied.

Angel stood to her feet. "Listen little girl, find you something safe to do."

Tabitha was about to get real verbal with the woman, but she thought about what happened the first time. And Val seemed nice compared to this one. "I tell you what, ma'am. If you call and tell him his sister Tab is here to see him, and he denies knowing me or doesn't want to see me, I'll leave. Deal?"

Angel smiled. "If he denies knowing you or if he refuses to see you, leaving will become a problem for you. Understood?"

"Fair enough," Tabitha agreed.

The smile faded from Angel's face. She pulled out her cellphone and called him. He picked up immediately.

"Sister, is everything okay? It's unlike you to call," Malice answered and said.

Angel kept an eye on Tabitha. "Brother, all is well. There's a youngster here to see you. She says she's your sister."

"Oh yeah? What's her name?" he asked.

"Her name is Tab," Angel replied.

"She's my flesh and blood. Make her feel comfortable. I'm on my way," Malice said.

"As you wish." Angel hung up. She stared into her eyes for a moment. "Follow me, Tab."

"Where are we going?" Tabitha asked.

"My brother's wishes are that I make you feel at home. He's in traffic, but he'll be here shortly. A little advice before he gets here though, don't become annoying to me unless you want to fight," Angel said provokingly.

She started walking, and Tabitha followed. She took her into the guild's training room. Being that it was a little past two, no one was there. No one but her and Angel, who closed and locked the door behind them.

Tabitha observed her body language. The woman didn't say a word. She sat on her knees, with her eyes closed, in the middle of the room. Angel no longer smiled, and everything about her looked to be radiating energy.

"Ma'am, what are you doing?" Tabitha asked, feeling uneasy.

"Technically, I'm minding my business. But, if you must know, I'm meditating. And stop calling me ma'am. My name is Angel," she said.

"I apologize," Tabitha said.

Angel sighed, irritated. "Tab, you're becoming annoying. I sense that you're a decent fighter, and I do enjoy a challenge. So, either you can be quiet, or we can spar. The choice is yours."

Normally, Tabitha would've been excited at a chance to spar, but Valencia took all that excitement away. "I think I'll pass on the sparring. I do have a question for you. Angel, are you a ninja?"

That did it for Angel. She opened her eyes before standing and unlocking the door. She took off the jacket and tossed it over in the corner. "Tab, you're going to learn to keep certain questions to yourself. Defend yourself."

As Angel walked towards her, Malice stepped through the door. "Halt!"

Angel stopped in her tracks. She turned towards him and bowed. "Brother."

He bowed back. "Sister." He looked at Tabitha and shook his head. "Tab, I think we're going to change your name to Suicide."

"We were about to spar," Tabitha said.

"Sparring with Angel is suicide. She's a real angel." Malice said and hugged Angel. "She's my angel. Her loyalty, love, life and honor is priceless. Excuse us, Angel."

Angel walked out of his embrace and out of the training room.

Tabitha noticed the photo album in his left hand. "What do you have there?" she asked curiously.

"Something some people, who will kill me if I don't bring you to meet them, wanted me to show you," he replied.

"Malice, did you murder my Uncle James Greene?" Tabitha asked.

He lowered his gaze. "Out of ignorance, yes, I did. After I was informed he was your uncle, I murdered the man who sent me to do it. And he was my Uncle Mickey, who was also your uncle."

Tabitha looked at him as if he'd suddenly grown two heads. "There must be some kind of mix-up. I don't have an uncle by the name of Mickey."

"Not anymore, you don't. Let me show you something." He opened the picture album and began explaining everything as it had been explained to him, while showing her the pictures of their family. "So, now you know the truth as it was told to me. Not to mention again, our grandmother is highly upset from never meeting you, especially since you were named after her mother. Now, it's your time to save my life from a grumpy old lady."

"I guess I can be of service to you this time," she said.

She held on to the picture book, flipping through the pages as they walked out.

CHAPTER ELEVEN

Angel and Trent had all of the members to meet in the training room after Malice and Tabitha left. They were reinforcing the traditional training rule when the knock came at the steel door. She motioned for one of them to see who it was while she continued to express the importance of training.

Just as were getting ready to dismiss, the young brother she'd sent to retrieve the message came flying back through the door, dripping blood everywhere. Next thing they knew, a group of red suit ninjas entered the room with their swords drawn. By the way they slaughtered most of the younger members, Angel and Trent could tell they were skilled in the dark arts.

The ninjas circled around them but restrained from attacking.

It all became clear when the rest of the ninjas filed into the room and lined the walls. The last one to enter spoke in Chinese to the ones surrounding them. They sheathed their swords and fell in the ranks with the others. He walked over to stand in the center of the room with Angel and Trent.

"I am Master Khan Tse Xan. Brother of Master Trion Li Xan, the master of this guild. Where is he?" he asked.

"I am Field Master Trent. It moves me deeply to inform you of the ill fate Master Trion suffered," Trent told him.

Master Khan Tse Xan grimaced. "Are you telling me my brother no longer lives?"

Trent and Angel lowered their gazes to the floor.

"Then who governs this guild? I would like to have a word with him," Khan demanded.

"Master Malice isn't here at the moment. He had some personal affairs that caused for his immediate attention," Trent said.

Master Khan looked around the room until his eyes fell upon Angel. "Daughter of the guild, what's your name?"

"Weapons Master Angel," she answered.

"Will you do me the honor of finding Master Malice? We'll be right here waiting on his presence," Khan added.

Angel bowed and hurried out. Outside, she jumped on the Kawasaki and spun out. She knew the lives of the others were in her timing. The only stop she made was at the red light.

Not trying to lose any leverage, she pulled out her cellphone and called him. The phone rang four times before he answered.

"I'm kind of in the middle of a family reunion. What's going on?" he said asked.

"While you're reuniting with one family, our family's being slaughtered," Angel replied in a harsh tone of voice.

"Slow down, Angel. What are you talking about?" Malice questioned her sternly.

"Trion's brother showed up with a welcoming party of reds. He seemed upset about the way things were being done. They're holding Trent and the others hostage until I return with you," she explained.

"Hold on for a second," he said.

Malice pulled Tabitha to the side. "Listen, we have to go now. There's trouble, and I'm not trying to lead it here. Do you know anywhere we can go and plan our attack?"

Tabitha nodded. "Yes, I do. Let's go."

Malice held the phone back to his ear. "Angel, stay on the line and track me by GPS."

"Gotcha," she replied.

Kenneth and Tabitha made up an excuse with a promise to return the following evening. Their grandparents bought it. On their way out to the car, he explained the situation. Tabitha got behind the wheel of the Mitsubishi and floored it.

They made it to the restaurant in record-setting time, and Angel pulled up shortly after. They drove around to the rear and parked, wanting to be discreet from the public.

Tabitha knocked on the backdoor, which was quickly opened by one of Saki's people. He looked out and surveyed the the scene. He wanted to make sure they hadn't been followed by unwanted company before shutting and locking the door behind them.

Sia, Saki, and Jennifer were amongst the warriors who were down in the basement. Kenneth saw Sia and bowed while greeting her in Chinese. She returned the greeting and bow to both he and Angel, who also responded in Chinese. Another surprise Tabitha hadn't known about.

Angel took the center floor. Everyone else stood or sat listening quietly. "The Triad has sent Khan Tse Xan to investigate the affairs of the late Trion Li Xan. He has come with a unit of Red Scorpions, the ninjas slaughtered the majority of our brothers and sisters of the guild. Only a few still survive, and their survival depends on Master Malice's presence being made before him. By Khan's affirmative action, I do believe he is here to take over the guild and return it to its traditional reason for being formed."

The mumbling under breaths begun as she finished. Sia, being the one used to handling such affairs, beckoned them to be silent. "I can honestly say, since Master Malice took control of the guild, the Po Clan has lived in peace more than chaos. However, I am no longer the head of the dragon. I'm its formidable tail. The decision of our assisting you is left to my cousin Saki."

She bowed towards her. Saki didn't take long to make her decision. Actually, she'd already decided to help them when she heard the Triad's involvement in the matter. All she wanted to know now was, how many assassins were with their master.

"Master Saki, there is a total of twenty-two. That includes Khan," Angel replied.

Saki nodded in deep thought. "Master Sia, prepare as many warriors as you think is needed."

Her cousin bowed before addressing fifteen of the Po Clan Warriors in Chinese. Then one-by-one, they made their departure.

Saki turned her attention to Tabitha. "Tabitha and Jennifer, you must remain here, where you will be safe. This isn't a fight that either of you would be of any help."

Neither attempted to object. Tabitha knew better, and Jennifer's silence was the reflection of her wisdom.

"Master Malice, I'm sure you added some additional unknown exit and entrance tunnels to the guild that no one, other than your most trusted, are aware of," Saki surmised.

His smile said it all.

"Great. Let's put it to use," she said.

Saki provided Malice and Angel with their weapons of choice. She even asked if they would like to change their attire, but they declined. Malice said he wanted his enemies to see who wield the blades of their death this time.

With everyone geared up, they left on foot.

Willie Slaughter

CHAPTER TWELVE

It was first dark when the force led by Malice and Saki reached the entrance to the secret tunnel. He drew the Dragon Blade and took the lead. Everyone else was in between he and Angel who closed up the rear. They moved through the tunnel at a quick pace because the lighting wasn't on their side.

After ten minutes of walking through the maze-like tunnel, they came to a halt at a door with a security pad on it. Although no one could see her, Sia nodded to show admiration for such a brilliant idea.

"This door opens up within my chambers, and no one can enter or exit without my retina and fingerprint," Malice explained.

He typed in the password and put his left eye up to the retina scanner. The door made a hissing sound as the lock slid and he pushed it open. They entered in quickly and moved about the room in attack formation. They needed to be sure their enemies hadn't found a way to breech the security system. But, thankfully, they hadn't.

Malice hurried over to the security monitors and turned them on. Just as he suspected, they were spread out in teams of three throughout the building.

Saki looked at the footage and frowned. She counted all twenty-one of the Red Scorpions along with their master, who sat alone inside of a room.

"Are they trying to lure us into a trap?" she asked.

"Why do you ask?" Malice asked in return.

"I'm counting all of them on screen. I'm trying to figure out why there's none on this wing of the building," she replied.

Malice pointed at the security footage. "This wing is a secured wing. It's our sleeping quarters. The only way to gain entry of any room to be the owner of that room. Unless you're an elders of the guild, you won't get access."

As he spoke, a brilliant thought entered his mind. "If I remember correctly, every room has a secret passageway that connects to all the other rooms as well as the tunnel we just walked through. We're twenty-one strong and we'll become even stronger once we take out the two teams holding Trent and the others hostage.

"Angel, you take Sia, and as many of the warriors you two will need, to your room. You know what to do from there," he concluded.

"My pleasure," Angel said.

He unlocked the door and they hurried out. He waited until she had entered her room and closed the door, before closing his own door.

Malice walked over to the wall opposite of the front door and pushed. The wall gave way under his weight and begin to turn inward. "Let's go," he summoned to the others.

With weapons already drawn, they passed through the wall into a smaller room-sized tunnel. The tunnel was designed with doors that had peepholes lining the walls.

He crept up to the one they had to enter and peered through the peephole. He could see the three Red

Scorpions standing in a circle around Trent. He closed his eyes to concentrate which allowed him to send Trent a telepathic message. When he reopen his eyes and looked through the peephole again, his brother was smiling and looking in his direction.

Without hesitation, Malice pushed through the door and rolled in their direction. His movement was so swift and silent, his enemies didn't see it coming until it was too late. He slashed, cutting the left leg off of the one closest to him, and before the other two could react, Saki and the others made a quick slaughter of them.

He finished the other one off by severing his head from his body. Trent didn't say a word. He bowed in respect to all present, picked up two of the swords, and followed suit of the others.

"Wait a moment," Malice said and closed his eyes to gain deeper focus. With his eyes closed, the vision of Angel and the Po Clan Warriors extracting the other team came to him. He also realized they were already advancing on the third team. When he saw Angel, Sia, and the combined forces slaughter the third team without suffering casualties of their own, he opened his eyes and smiled. "Alright, coast is clear. Let's continue forward," he instructed.

Their forces together were too formidable for the Red Scorpions. They murdered them in some of the most heinous ways, mutilating them, sending a sure message to any who dared to challenge their might. All seven of the Red Scorpions' teams had fallen, and the only one left was their master.

Malice sheathed his bloodstained sword and started for the training room door.

Saki stepped in front him, stopping him short of his entry. "For our assistance, I ask that you honor this one request, Master Malice. Allow me the honor to serve justice on this master. As you've avenged the death of your family, don't deny me the right to avenge mines. However, you are all welcomed to watch."

"Master Saki Po, I gladly honor your request," Malice said and did a quick bow of confirmation. In turn, she returned the salute.

CHAPTER THIRTEEN

The Po Clan, along with Malice and his group of mercenaries, stood around the wall inside the training room with their swords drawn. Saki stood in the center facing the Red Scorpion, Master Khan.

"Master Khan, I am Master Saki Po. I challenge you to martial combat. We will fight without weapons until there's no breath left within our bodies. If you choose to dishonor me by not accepting this challenge, I will dismember you limb-by-limb in a very slow and painful way."

She laid her sword and daggers down on the floor before her. Khan took off the mask, revealing his face. He spoke harshly in Chinese before launching an attack with his sword. Quickly, she picked her sheathed sword up and blocked.

The outraged master was all out in his attack. Saki sidestepped, rolled under and blocked his every attempt without unsheathing her blade. He tried to fake a thrust with the sword and came with a side high kick. She countered by swiping the blade outward while simultaneously drawing her sword. She slashed into his upper right thigh twice, causing him to stumble backwards.

The memory of her mother and father's death settled into the forefront of her consciousness. Saki went from defense to offense, and the Red Scorpion Master proved to be of no match for her. She delivered every cutting blow with precision. Not only did she dismember him, she cut his intestines out as well.

With the battle over, everyone on the wall raised their swords in a mighty warrior's salute.

Saki raised hers in response and spoke. "As we've worked together to destroy the wickedness that came forth, let us work together to clean this place up and continue to crush our common enemies at their arrival."

Everybody touched the hilt of their sword to their chest and raised it in salute, sealing their pact.

Afterwards, they begin to clean up the blood and dead corpses. There were a great many which had to be picked up limb-by-limb. It had truly been a slaughter inside the slaughterhouse.

They walked out into the coolness of the night and down into the terminal where everyone boarded the Amtrak. No one was really up for conversation, and it showed through the silence. Nonetheless, there was one question left unanswered and Sia needed to know the answer.

"Master Malice, I have a question for you." Sia said.

"Hopefully, I'll be able to answer it. What is it, Master Sia?" Malice replied.

"Who is Tabitha Greene?" she asked.

"She's my flesh and blood. The daughter of Terrance Greene and my Aunty Martha Freeman," he answered.

Sia nodded. "Hmm . . . Interesting. So, will she be training in the dark arts?"

"Master Sia, I was hoping you would all manage her training, since your clan is the balance to the darkness," he proposed.

"Wise decision, Master Malice. If she will accept our invitation, we will accept her as our sister," Sia said, in a welcoming tone.

Malice bowed. "I will be most grateful, Master Sia. I do have one request," he told her.

"What might this request be?" she asked.

"That you will train her harder than you train everyone else. She's an heir of our families' estates and much more. She must be prepared to defend herself and her heritage at all times," he said.

She bowed honorably and replied, "As you wish."

The silence returned. Each person was caught in the web of their own thoughts. They made it to their destination without any unwanted attention. The rest of the Po Clan, along with Tabitha and Jennifer, had been sitting in the restaurant area waiting on their return.

When they went through the door, it was as if a cool breeze had entered with them. The sighs of relief could be heard throughout the silence of area.

Tabitha jumped up and ran to Kenneth and embraced him knowingly. Turning her attention on Angel, she hugged her as well.

Surprisingly, she returned the affection, but not without a sense of humor. She now understood that Tabitha was one of them, she was family. "Tab, I know my brother has enlightened you on the sentimental jargon. We can be sisters without the touchiness. Besides, you have a girlfriend, and I have a man I love," she said with a crooked smile.

She walked up to Kenneth and kissed him passionately. At first he was shocked, but then he couldn't help but in. Jennifer tugged on Tabitha's sleeve. She knew that was her cue and she was ready to go home.

Tabitha exhaled deeply. "Well, this has been a historical day. We'll see you guys tomorrow," she told everyone as she and Jennifer stood to leave.

"Not just yet, Tabitha. You have a decision to make," Saki said, causing Tabitha to stop in midstride.

She looked at Saki questioningly.

"We would be honored to have you join our clan as a sister. You will be acknowledged as a Po amongst your other heritage," Saki said.

Tabitha didn't know how to respond. A family had been taken from her. Now, another was ready to give birth to her. She looked back at Kenneth who nodded, a broad smile fixated on his face. Even Angel gave her a thumbs up.

"I accept your offer, Saki. I will call first thing tomorrow morning and resign from the bureau. I see now, I'm able to do more in the shadows than in the light," Tabitha said.

Saki bowed, and she bowed back.

"Alright, Tab. Don't forget we promised the old folks we were visiting them tomorrow evening," Malice reminded her.

As she and Jennifer made their exit, she threw up the peace sign in response to his reminder.

Once seated inside the Porsche, Jennifer leaned over in the passenger seat and kissed her hungrily. "You don't know how long I've been waiting to do that."

"No longer than I've anticipated it," Tabitha said. She pushed the ignition button, and the car's engine came to life.

Jennifer turned on the radio. Coincidently, *Dangerously In Love* was the song playing. She turned up the volume and looked over at Tabitha. "This is definitely our song, babes."

Tabitha shook her head and smiled happily. She pulled out of the lot of the restaurant into the moving traffic.

Malice, Angel, and Trent had left shortly after Tabitha and Jennifer. Arriving at the slaughterhouse, they entered the building. Angel flipped the sorry we're closed sign around so that it faced inward. Trent and Malice sat down at the counter, neither saying a word. She sat down on the stool between them. Her thoughts were on Valencia, someone who she'd loved like a big sister.

"It's not the same around here without Val," she said solemnly.

Trent nodded slowly revealing his own feelings of sadness. "Yeah, Valencia is definitely missed. She was a true bloodthirsty sister. A sister true to the guild." He draped his arm around Angel's shoulders. "Never think I don't feel or understand your pain, sis."

Angel held the tears inside. It was a struggle, but she managed to remain calm. "I will show mercy to whoever was responsible for killing my sister."

"I'm with you, Angel," Trent promised.

Malice sat in silence, hearing the weariness within their voices as they spoke of Valencia. His pain was greater than theirs because beneath his pain was guilt and disloyalty— something he'd never felt until killing Valencia. The memory of the fight played over and over in his mind.

"Excuse me," he said, before standing up and walking off.

Trent nor Angel attempted to stop him or ask where he was going. They could see his pain in his body language.

Malice walked to the training room and posted up against the wall with tears flowing from his eyes. His pain was greater than he could understand.

So caught up in his emotional moment, he wasn't aware of Angel's presence in the room until she spoke. "Malice. . . are you okay?" she asked. Now, she was even more concerned because she had never witnessed him in tears. He was strong man, a man of power, yet everyone failed to realize he was also human.

He wiped his eyes. "Yeah, I'm good. Just releasing the tensions that comes with facing reality.

She walked up to him and hugged him tightly. She released her firm embrace and stared into his eyes. "True enough, Valencia is gone, but we have gained a lot in her death."

He nodded his understanding because he knew exactly what she was referring to. *If only she knew why I'm in such an emotional state . . . her affection would probably turn to murderous intentions towards me,* Malice thought to himself.

Willie Slaughter

CHAPTER FOURTEEN

Meanwhile, on the other side of the globe in Beijing, China, General Chan Chou sat in his office at the police station. He was anticipating a phone call from some associates of his. He'd paid them a handsome amount of funds to take care of a situation in America. They had made contact with him when they arrived at the airport. But, since then, he hadn't heard from them.

Haven grown restless from the wait, General Chan picked up his phone from off the desk. *Since they haven't called me, I might as well call them,* he thought as he looked through the contacts on his phone. He found the contact he was looking for and placed the call him. There was no answer, so the voicemail picked up instead.

Now, there was only one conclusion to be drawn. As Po Clan sat and contemplated his sudden dilemma he had a sudden thought . . . *Po Clan had proven to be the greatest clan of warriors.* And with that thought in mind, he dialed another number and relaxed in his chair when she answered.

"Hello? Master Ma Sune speaking," the woman said.

Chan kicked his feet up on the desk. "Master Ma Sune, this is General Chan Chou. I was wondering when you would be available to meet with me."

"When I have the free time, I'll be sure to give you a call, General Chan Chou. Until then, have a great day," Ma Sune said, and hung up without further conversing.

Such arrogance infuriated Chan, but he knew he had no choice but to accept the disrespect she dished out or die trying to defend his respect. Although arrogant in her ways, Ma Sune was a very powerful woman. When it came to the way of Ninja, the Sune Clan was right behind the Po Clan. No other clan matched them in martial skills or weapon proficiency. They were the best of the best.

General Chan smiled to himself. He knew if he could form an alliance with the Sune Clan, he would have a greater chance of defeating the Po Clan. Without their assistance, his chances were non-existent. The Brown Locusts weren't a match for Black Dragon nor Green Mantis.

***

Ma Sune had summoned her daughter Yishi after she'd gotten off the phone with the general. She walked into the study and bowed. Ma Sune returned the bow and requested her to have a seat. Yishi sat down and waited silently for her mother to state her reason for summoning her.

"Young Master Yishi, we have a little problem," Ma Sune said.

Yishi breathed heavily. She understood what her mother was getting at but inquired anyway. "What is it, Mother?"

"General Chan Chou has requested our assistance concerning a matter," she stated.

Her daughter looked at her questioningly. "And what matter would that be?"

"He didn't really say," Ma Sune replied.

"Well, are you going to extend a helping hand to whatever cause it might be?" Yishi asked.

Ma Sune thought about what Yishi was really asking. It wasn't a question of how much assistance she was willing to give, but what the end result would be.

"We'll cross that bridge when we get to it," she said, "until then, I need for you to do some scouting. See what you can find out. Something's telling me General Chan Chou is up to no good," she added.

Yishi stood up and bowed. "Will that be all Mother?"

"Yes, Young Master Yishi, that will be all," she replied.

"I shall be on my way then," she said before turning around and leaving out of the study.

Ma Sune relaxed in the chair. She found herself pondering over previous outcomes. Once she'd seen each thought to its true destination, she closed her eyes and sat in meditation.

Yishi took to the shadows. She scaled rooftop after rooftop, making her way to her destination. Dressed in a forest green ninja suit, it was hard for anyone to spot her in the darkness. Upon reaching her destination, she took a couple of deep breaths before she began snooping around.

General Chan Chou sat in his office at the station pondering his next move. When his private line began ringing, he picked up the receiver. "General Chan Chou speaking," he said in Chinese.

"General Chan Chou, this is Headmaster Hia Xan Tu. You have the vote in your favor of the High Council's assistance in the matter," Hia said and hung up.

Chan replaced the receiver on the phone. He leaned back in his chair with a smile upon his face. In his mind, he had already won the war. He would finally destroy the Po Clan and unite with the Sune Clan. And together, The Green Mantises and Brown Locusts would take down the High Council.

General Chan Chou felt victorious. He closed his eyes and allowed the thoughts of victory to take shape within his mind. Every image that took form made the smile on his face widen. *My rule has come*, he thought to himself.

***

Hia Xan Tu, the Headmaster of the High Council, sat comfortably in his chair at the head of the council table. His subordinates, sat in silence, awaiting on him to state the nature of the emergency meeting he'd called. Hia called in his informant and commanded him to give his report before them.

After the young man had given his report, he stood silently, waiting on the next set of instructions from his master.

"Thank you, young man. You have served this High Council well, however, your services are no longer needed," Hia stated. He nodded to the unseen assassin lurking in the shadows.

Right before them, the assassin quickly severed the young man's head from his body. No one ever saw the assassin. All they had seen was the glint of steel slice through the air.

"Now, to get on with this meeting. The Po Clan, who are in the United States of America, have proven to be stronger in numbers than General Chan Chou thought. He has asked for the assistance of this council. We shall vote as it is within the tradition of The High Council," Hia said.

He stood to his feet and looked around the council table. He could see the fear within the body language of some. They were still shaken by the death of the young informant.

"Council members let not the death of an inferior bother you so. We are all due to death sooner or later. Now, all in favor of assisting The Brown Locust Clan, raise your left hand," Hia commanded, in a nonchalant tone of voice.

Whether out of fear or not, the majority of them raised their left hands. Out of the thirteen, only two hands remained lowered. One of those hands belonged to the headmaster, himself.

"It is settled. Those in favor of assisting General Chan Chou, do as you feel. Just remember, The Black Dragon Clan is the most formidable foe you will ever face. None have faced them and lived to tell the story," Headmaster Hia Xan Tu said, remembering what it was like sparring with Master Han Xi Po. It was the most physical, painful experience he'd gone through daily.

"This emergency meeting is adjourned," he said. He remained standing until the other council members were gone.

Hia motioned for the deadly assassins to come out of the shadows. Swiftly, two of them stepped into the dim candlelit room and cleaned up the dead corpse. The headmaster sat back in his chair in deep thought. He knew the other council members were headed for destruction, but, to him, they were replaceable, so it didn't matter.

***

Saki called her brother, Qi Dom Po, who was living in Beijing amongst the other Po Clan who were in hiding. It had been a while since she had last spoken with him. Especially with all the bloodshed surrounding her. She really didn't want anyone to know they were still in contact with one another.

She placed the international phone call and paid the fee. The phone rang twice before he answered.

"Hello? Qi speaking," he answered and said.

"Brother, it is I, Saki Po. How are you?"

"Saki! I'm so happy to hear from you," he exclaimed.

Hearing the excitement in his voice let her know her little brother was okay. "Same here, Qi Dom Po. Do you need anything?"

"Umm . . . Not exactly. But I guess you could send me some funds," Qi replied, not wanting to make his sister feel as if he was refusing her offer.

"Okay, I'm wiring you $500 in the morning. And Qi, once all of this is over, we shall reunite under the same roof. I swear," Saki promised.

They talked for a thirty minutes. Mostly about what was going on in Beijing because she didn't care to tell him about the troubles she'd been facing.

"Alright, Qi Dom Po, I'll talk with you later. I love you," Saki said before hanging up. She relaxed in bed, thinking about the possible troubles ahead of her, and her family and allies.

***

Qi Dom Po traveled his usual route back to the hideout. The talk with his sister had made him so happy his senses weren't as sharp as they normally would've been. As he walked through the back alleyways in the dark, the assassin dressed in the midnight blue ninja suit tailed him from the rooftops. The assassin's silent and swift movement was flawless.

Qi Dom Po approached the entrance of the Po Clan's hideout. Finally, his sense of awareness kicked back in, causing him to stop and look towards the rooftops. "You can come out and attempt to do what your master has sent you to do." Calmly, he had spoken in the language of Mandarin.

The assassin flipped from the rooftop and landed silently on his feet a yard away from Qi. He immediately unsheathed his sword and initiated an attack. He wielded the deadly blade expertly, but to no avail. Every attack he tried, Qi Dom Po evaded effortlessly.

The assassin launched in with a thrusting attack, which Qi Dom Po countered by spinning left and hitting his opponent with a crushing right spinning back fist to the back of the head. The assassin stumbled forward, but quickly regained his composure. He tried another thrust attack. Instead of trying to evade, this time Qi Dom Po leapt into the air and kicked him in the face with a spinning roundhouse kick.

The assassin went down hard, dropping his sword. Qi Dom Po picked it up. "Now, let me show you how it is done," he said in his native language before launching an attack on the assassin.

The silent killer didn't fall easily. He evaded the first slash and thrust attack. But the relentlessness of Qi Dom Po's forward motion was too much for him. Qi went into a whirlwind attack, causing the assassin to turn a series of backward flips.

As he landed on his feet, Qi Dom Po did an upward slash maneuver. The instrument of death cut through the assassin's torso, causing him to fall to the asphalt writhing in pain.

"I would ask you who sent you, but I know it is pointless," he said. Without hesitating, he thrust the blade through the assassin's throat and twisted it.

The assassin's body spasm as the steel claimed his life. Qi Dom Po drug the lifeless corpse behind a dumpster.

Afterwards, he entered through the secret passage, took a shower, and lay down. *Will this war ever be over?* He closed his eyelids and allowed rest to claim his tired body.

***

A couple of weeks passed, and Tabitha found herself visiting her uncle's gravesite. She didn't attend the funeral because funerals just weren't her thing. Because it was the same place the rest of the Greene's had been buried, she decided to pay her respects to her mother and father as well. She had only bought a dozen of black, red, and white roses, so she ended up putting a rose on each grave she stopped in front of.

"I miss you so much," Tabitha said at a whisper, as she knelt before her mother and father's tombstones which were side-by-side. Her tears freed themselves and began rolling down her cheeks. As she sat on her haunches crying, Malice walked over and sat next to her.

"Let it out, cousin," he said, as he grabbed her and held her close. "It's alright."

Tabitha buried her face in his shoulder. "I'm so alone in this fucked up world," she cried. Her words were being muffled by his shoulder, but he was able to make out what she'd said.

"No, you're not, Tab. You have me, our grandparents, and as surprising as this may sound, Angel. She just has a strange way of expressing her likes and dislikes," he explained.

His sense of humor made her laugh. "Yeah, I can go for that, seeing how much she enjoys expressing her dislikes."

"I can't disagree with you there," Malice replied. Then, out of nowhere, an eerie feeling came over him, as if they were being watched. "Tab, we got to get out of the open. We're sitting targets if we stay here."

Before Tabitha could ask Malice what was going on, she found herself pushing him to the ground. The ninja stars whizzed by her, missing her head by no more than a centimeter.

Quickly, they rolled behind the three foot tall tombstones of her parents' graves. Adrenaline rushing, they looked around, trying to locate the unseen hands that had threw the stars.

"At your 2 o'clock," Malice said, while pointing at a six foot tall grave marker.

Tabitha peeped and noticed part of the assassin's foot was visible. She leaned back against the tombstone and gave Malice the thumbs up. "Yeah, I see them. That's a good distance from where we are."

"Yeah, I know. We're going to use it to our advantage. When I count to three, I want you to run zigzag as fast as you can towards the cars. I'm going to use that time to reach them and . . . You know the rest," Malice replied.

Tabitha nodded. "Alright. I'm ready when you are."

"One. Two. Three!" he counted.

Tabitha ran exactly how he'd instructed her to. The silent instruments of death cut through the air, whizzing by her on both sides. Malice stayed low to the ground but moved at a fast pace towards the assassin hiding behind the grave marker. Before the assassin knew what was happening, it was too late for him.

Malice tucked and rolled right up on the assassin dressed in the tan brown ninja suit. He came to his feet with an elbow uppercut to the assassin's chin. Before the assassin could stumble or regain his footing, Malice snapped his neck like a twig.

Tabitha made it to where their cars were parked. She was greeted by Angel, who had her right foot on the throat of one of the assassins. "For the record," Angel began saying as she crushed the assassin's windpipe with the 6 inch heel, "you are not a public figure anymore, Tabitha. So, do us all a favor. Stop being so damn careless."

Malice came trotting up on the scene. The first thing he noticed was, the dead corpse under Angel's foot. He nodded to her. "Nice work, luv. Let's get the hell out of here before more show up," he said.

Tabitha didn't hesitate to jump behind the wheel of her Audi 8. Malice and Angel waited on her to drive off before tailing her closely.

"Your cousin better shape up real fast before she find herself being fertilizer. I ain't got time to be playing savior, Malice. I swear," Angel said.

By her tone of voice, Malice knew she wasn't joking. "I understand, Angel. Saki will tighten her up," he replied.

They rode in silence the rest of the way back to Jersey City, New Jersey. They followed Tabitha all the way to Saki's restaurant. Once she was safely inside, Malice pulled off.

Tabitha sat down on a stool in front of the cash register, and behind it stood Sia. She took one good look at Tabitha and realized her day had been rough. "Tabitha is there anything I can get you?" asked Sia.

The adrenaline rush she had experienced earlier had given her an appetite. "Whatever special you have for the day will be fine, Sia," Tabitha replied.

"Coming right up," Sia said, before yelling to the cooks in Mandarin.

Tabitha buried her face in her folded arms, on the counter. The only thing she could think of was the scene at the cemetery. . . . *the ninja stars whizzing by her head, just centimeters away from claiming her life . . .*

"Tabitha is everything okay with you?" asked a familiar feminine voice.

She'd been so wrapped up in her thoughts she didn't know Saki had walked up and sat beside her. "If having assassins trying to kill you on a regular basis constitutes being okay, then I'm great. If not, then I'm fucking irritated," Tabitha answered without lifting her head.

"I take it, you've had an interesting day. Care to talk about it?" she probed.

Tabitha gave Saki and Sia the rundown on what had happened at the cemetery. They listened with looks of concern on their faces.

"Maybe we should start your training, Tabitha. Enjoy your meal and meet us down in the basement once your food has settled," Saki said. She got up and walked to the back, giving orders in her native language.

"See you downstairs, Tabitha," Sia said, as she was relieved of her duty by an elderly woman. The woman brought Tabitha her food and sat it in front of her on the counter.

Smelling the fresh scent of the oven baked clams, egg rolls, sweet and tangy soy sauce, and fried shredded cabbage, Tabitha's head shot up. She went to work on the meal.

"Take your time, child," the elderly woman said.

Tabitha paused long enough to acknowledge her by nodding. She then returned her focus to the task of eating the delicious dish they'd prepared for her.

Done eating, she paid the tab. On her way down to the basement, she took the empty plates on the platter to the dishwashers.

Saki, Sia, and three other members of the Po Clan were sitting in meditation when she showed up.

Tabitha sat in the lotus position between Saki and Sia. They sat for thirty minutes before prostrating and standing to their feet.

"Sister Tabitha, you have made the conscious decision to become a sister of the Po Clan. Now, you must start training as we train. Are you ready?" Saki asked, revealing no sign of emotion whatsoever.

Tabitha bowed towards Saki. "Yes, I'm ready, Master Saki Po."

"Hmm . . . Normally, one does not get to choose their training partner. Since you do not understand our customs, I'm willing to let you choose, Tabitha. Of course, you know who Master Sia Po is. This is Master Mi Nu Po," Saki said.

Master Mi Nu Po bowed, and Tabitha bowed back. She was four feet eleven, weighed one hundred eight pounds, had a dark bronze skin complexion, and long silky black hair that reached the small of her back. Mi was thirty years old but didn't look a day over sixteen.

"This is Master Zoe Mae Po," Saki said, as she gestured in Zoe's direction.

Zoe Mae Po was five feet tall, one hundred thirteen pounds, with a dark bronze skin complexion and long silky black hair. She was around the same age as Tabitha. She bowed, and Tabitha bowed back.

"And last, but not least amongst us in skill, this is Master Fae Dao Po," Saki said, making the final introduction.

Fae bowed. She was one hundred pounds, if that much, four feet eight inches tall, with dark bronze skin, and long silky black hair that reached her waistline. To Tabitha, she looked to be no more than nineteen years old.

"So, who shall it be, Sister Tabitha?" asked Saki, whose facial expression never seemed to change.

Noticing she was having a hard time deciding, Sia decided for her. "Master Zoe Mae Po and Tabitha, front and center."

Everyone else stepped back and took a seat on a plush cushion.

"There is no retreat, Tabitha. You must stand toe to toe and face your opponent. The match is not over until you successfully strike Master Zoe Mae Po. Understood?" Sia quizzed.

Tabitha nodded in the affirmative. *How hard can it be to land a single punch,* she thought.

"Ready," Sia called out, prompting the two women to touch the back of their right hands together. "Begin."

The training began and if there ever was a time for her to make her uncle proud, now was the time.

Zoe and Tabitha begin to circle around with their hands still touching. The confidence reflecting from Zoe's eyes told Tabitha an unknown truth. *Man, I believe I've bitten off more than I can chew,* she thought. And her thoughts served her well when Zoe decided to strike.

With lightning fast speed, Zoe struck Tabitha on the right jaw with her left hand. She then rolled her right wrist, grabbing hold of Tabitha's, and hip tossed her onto the floor. She stood back, allowing her time to get back on her feet to reset the match.

Never being the one to give up, Tabitha sprung to her feet and placed her right hand against Zoe's again.

Time after time after time, she was picking herself up off the floor. Feeling the pain after the seventh time down, it took her a minute to get up. Saki realized Tabitha's chance of hitting Zoe was zero. She inhaled and exhaled deeply and tapped Sia on the arm. Sia, understood just what this meant and called the match.

"Halt! That's enough sparring for the moment. Sister Tabitha what did you learn from this experience?" Sia asked, in an effort to examine her understanding.

Wincing from the pain, Tabitha hobbled over to a chair and sat down. She had to catch her breath before speaking. "I've learned to never underestimate a person because of their size. And I definitely learned I need a lot of training if I'm going to live through this feud."

"Wise choice of words. Well, let's get you home. Sia will drive your car and you will ride with me," Saki replied.

Saki, Sia, and Tabitha left out through the basement door. They got Tabitha home safely. Jennifer had met her at the front door with worry written over her face.

"Oh my God! Tabby, what happened to you? Are you okay? I thought you were gone to visit your parents' graves," Jennifer said.

Tabitha limped inside. "I did that too, Jenn," she replied.

"Well damn, the dead must have decided to rise and kick your ass," Jennifer said sarcastically.

She laughed and replied, "Yeah, something like that. Listen, Jenn, it's been a rough day. All I want to do is take a hot bath and go to sleep."

"Well, that ruined my plans for us, Tabby," Jennifer said, seemingly disappointed.

For the first time, Tabitha ignored her and turned to head to the bathroom. She turned on the bathwater and sat down in the tub. The steaming water was so relaxing, she would've fallen asleep if it hadn't been for hearing the sound of Jennifer's voice as she entered the bathroom.

"Tabby, what really happened?" asked Jennifer.

"Training is what happened, Jenn," she replied. She reached for the sponge and body wash, but Jennifer grabbed it for her.

"Relax. Let me take care of you, Tabby," Jennifer said, as she began washing Tabitha's body gently. As she descended to her breasts, she lightened her touch and circled around Tabitha's exposed nipples. The sensation of her touch caused her to sigh and moan simultaneously.

"That's right, hon . . . let me take good care of you," Jennifer coached again in a lustful tone of voice. She rubbed down her body with the sponge. After washing between Tabitha's thighs, she let go of the sponge and inserted two fingers inside of Tabitha's natural flower. She leaned over and kissed her lips while she stroked her insides with her fingers slowly.

"Mm, Jenn." Tabitha moaned at a whisper.

"Yes, baby?" Jenn responded in between kisses.

She tongue-kissed Tabitha while thrusting her fingers deeper inside of her. As the release continued to build, Tabitha began thrusting herself harder on Jennifer's fingers. She moaned and thrust faster, and her moans became louder, until finally her body quaked from the release.

"Oh, Jenn. Baby, why do you have to be so demanding of my love?" Tabitha said. Her lips quivered from the passionate release.

"Because I love you so much, Tabby. Now, let's finish bathing you and get you in bed. You'll feel better in the morning after a good breakfast in bed," Jennifer replied. She resumed bathing her with the sponge and body wash.

Tabitha relaxed and allowed her to take total control. She really didn't want to have sex at the moment. Her thoughts were on learning how to defend herself as well as those she loved, against ninjas. *Something you haven't the first clue of how to do Jenn,* Tabitha thought as Jennifer continued to bathe her and fulfill her own lustful desires at the same time.

She was thankful when it was over, and she was left alone in bed to rest. Sleep claimed her battered and bruised body instantly. She woke up the next morning to breakfast in bed just like Jennifer had promised. While she ate, her thoughts returned back to focusing on training and surviving.

***

General Chan Chou sat in his office at the station pondering his next move, when his private line began ringing. He picked up the receiver. "General Chan Chou speaking," he answered in Chinese.

"General Chan Chou, this is Headmaster Hia Xan Tu. You have the vote in your favor of the High Council's assistance in the matter," Hia said and hung up.

Chan replaced the receiver on the phone. He leaned back in his chair with a smile on his face. In *his* mind, he had already won the war. He would finally destroy the Po Clan and unite with the Sune Clan. And together, The Green Mantises and Brown Locusts would take down the High Council.

General Chan Chou felt victorious. He closed his eyes and allowed the thoughts of victory to take shape within his psyche. Every image that took form made the smile on his face widen. *My rule has come*, he thought.

***

Saki and the rest of the Po Clan were in the middle of their morning meditation when Tabitha arrived. She stood on the bottom step in the basement, watching Sia lead the meditation. It was almost magical seeing how flexible and precise she was. She performed every pose to the perfection.

Upon ending the morning ritual, Sia prostrated, and everyone else followed her lead. In Mandarin, Saki commanded everyone to go and prepare to fulfill their duties.

Everyone bowed as they passed Tabitha on the steps. Out of respect, she bowed back.

Saki and Sia remained standing in the basement. Tabitha walked over to the center of the room where they stood. "Good morning, Saki and Sia." Tabitha bowed as she greeted them.

Instead of engaging in formalities with Tabitha, Sia attacked her, using pressure point strikes. Tabitha found herself unable to feel her arms, and when she tried to defend herself against another one of Sia's assaults, she realized her arms were useless.

"Tabitha, it is the Touch of the Dragon, or for your understanding, pressure point manipulation," Sia said while continuing her frontal assault. "All I'm doing is, identifying every point on your body that allows me to dominate you with little effort. A technique that will work against any size opponent."

Tabitha realized she was in no condition to fight back or defend herself, so she did the next best thing. She evaded as best as her aching body would allow. However, Sia didn't stop her attack.

"Understand the reaction to being struck in these points, in order to effectively plan combinations for counters and offensive attacks. This is how you use the body's natural defense system to strike pressure points effectively." Sia instructed her while administering just enough pressure so Tabitha would feel the effects.

Without warning, she changed her style of attack. She grabbed Tabitha's extended arm and applied pressure at the joint, causing her to wince from the pain she was feeling. "Another Touch of the Dragon. But this specific touch is for joint manipulation. I'm simply using comprehension and hyperextension tactics of the joints to subdue you."

Tabitha finally managed to get her arm free of Sia's deadly grasp. She attempted to throw a left jab. Sia caught her fist in mid swing, but before she could counter, Tabitha used her right hand to wrap Sia up in a choke hold. Sia dropped straight to the floor and used an open palm strike, hitting Tabitha at the inner right knee, causing her to stumble off balance.

"Joint manipulation can also be used to escape holds, using simple moves like this that require no strength. Basically, ground fighting without having to wrestle," Sia said, as she stood from the crouching position.

Saki watched the training in silence. She found pleasure in watching Sia teach Tabitha the way of the Black Dragon— the forward, side, circling, hooking, backward, sweeping, and leaping movements. She taught her how to master the hand and foot techniques, mastering the body posture and shadow, defending the circle, trapping within the circle, and cuffing through the circle.

"Tabitha, the Black Dragon Spirit is within your heart and mind. You must understand the animal within you. That way, you master the animal's movements and nature. All in all, you become the Black Dragon," Sia said.

Tired, beaten and bruised, Tabitha nodded. "Understood. And thank you for the training, Master Sia."

"Oh, it is necessary, but you are welcome. Let's continue," Sia replied.

They worked on her balance, mobility, striking power, ability to withstand stress, hands, feet and torso coordination, intuitiveness, instinctive distancing, and relaxed agile movement stimulation of self-testing energy and internal power.

Although Tabitha was getting her ass kicked, she felt herself growing stronger. *I'll be glad when this session is over,* she thought, feeling the pain Sia had administered effortlessly.

"Alright, Master Sia, Sister Tabitha has experienced enough for the moment," Saki said.

Sia ceased in her forward movement. Tabitha was so thankful she bowed three times instead of the usual one. Sia had to stifle a laugh. Saki, on the other hand, maintained a straight face.

"Please, utilize the baths we have here. After you have freshened up, join us upstairs for a morning meal," Saki said. She made her way up the stairs, leaving Sia and Tabitha to bathe.

They took turns in the shower and afterwards, Sia grabbed Tabitha some fresh clothes to put on. When she entered the shower room to sit the clothes down, she paused, seeing Tabitha naked.

"Excuse me," Sia said.

"It's okay," Tabitha replied and took the clothes out of her hands. She dressed in front of Sia who stood watching speechless. After she finished, they walked up stairs and joined Saki and the others for the morning meal.

During the morning meal, Sia and Tabitha eyed each other the whole while. Nobody spoke because it was their custom not to speak while eating. They ate fried salmon patties, fried cornbread patties, scrambled tofu, and raw honey. They drank unsweetened herbal tea to wash it down, which did miracles for Tabitha. The food and drink had worked its magic on her sore muscles.

After everyone had eaten their share of the delicious food, the tables were cleared and cleaned, and everybody prepared to open up the restaurant to the public. Tabitha helped out in the dishwashing room even though she knew cooking, waitressing, and clerical work was not her thing.

As she removed the China wear from the dishwasher, her cellphone ringtone icon started playing. She put the dishes where the young Asian man instructed her to and dried off her hands before answering the call. Since the caller hadn't hung up and tried to call back, she knew it was Jennifer.

"What's up, Jenn? Shouldn't you be taking calls instead of making calls?" asked Tabitha. She could hear Jennifer giggle.

"Yeah, you are so right, Tabby. But incoming calls are slow at the moment, so I decided to call and check on my wifey," Jennifer replied.

"I'm good. We're opening up at the restaurant. On that note, I'm going to have to take a raincheck on lunch today," she said.

Jennifer sighed, irritated by the lack of quality time she and Tabitha neglected to have ever since she'd become acquainted with the Po Clan and her family. "Alright. I guess I'll see you when you get home."

"Probably be running late, so you don't have to wait up. Love you, Jenn," Tabitha said and hung up. She returned to her duties. Every so often, Sia would walk through, checking to see how she was doing. But the look in her eyes said much more to Tabitha. And for some reason, she felt herself willing to explore more with her.

***

After a long tiresome day, she'd finally made it home around midnight. Although she had told Jennifer not to wait up for her, she did. Instead of giving her time to start rambling off about coming in so late, Tabitha gave her a quick peck on the lips. She walked into the bedroom, undressed, and got in bed.

Jennifer didn't miss anything. She noticed Tabitha wasn't wearing the same clothes she'd left home wearing that day.

"Tabby, did you go shopping and decide to throw away the clothes you wore this morning? Tabby?" she said again.

"Goodnight, Jenn." Tabitha responded and fell asleep.

***

Malice, Angel, and Trent were screening the new members of the guild when the alarm went off, signaling there was someone entering the slaughterhouse, armed. Trent pulled the security footage of the entrance up on his iPhone.

"Yo, Malice, you might want to take a look at this."

Malice, along with Angel at his side, looked at the footage on Trent's iPhone. What they saw were four Chinese men dressed in tan business suits sitting at the counter. Neither looked to be over thirty years old.

"Strap up and let's go give them a warm welcome. Any sudden moves, we take them out," Malice said.

They walked out of the training room and into the store front with Malice leading the way. As soon as the four Chinese men spotted them, they stood and bowed. Malice noticed one of them was wearing a gold chain with a gold locust pendant dangling from it. He was the one who chose to speak.

"Is this the guild led by Master Malice?"

"I am Master Malice. How can I help you?" Malice replied with a straight face.

"Master Malice, I am Junior Master Nom Pi Chou of the Brown Locust Clan. I do believe this guild belongs to us, therefore, I am here to oversee the affairs of this guild to make sure it is serving the purpose we created it for," Nom stated.

"Hmm . . . I see. Now, exactly what is this purpose you are speaking of, Junior Master Nom Pi Chou?" Malice retorted. He looked behind him at the members of the guild and turned back around to face Nom and his subordinates. "Because we would like to know."

"Very well, Master Malice. This guild is a mercenary outpost of the Brown Locust Clan, purposed to kill every Po Clan member who are our sworn enemies There are reports stating this guild has not been serving this purpose. That is why I am here now," Nom replied.

Malice smiled, thinking about what the man had said. "Interesting. Now, can I give you my report, Junior Master Nom Pi Chou? It's not lengthy."

"Of course, Master Malice. I will be more than honored to deliver the report to my uncle," Nom answered.

Malice walked up on the man. Seeing their leader's reaction, Angel, Trent, and the others readied themselves for battle. "Junior Master Nom Pi Chou, my report is to chop," he said, as the ninja star he'd concealed cut through the man's jugular vein. Malice did a spinning heel kick, sending the already dying man flying off his feet backwards.

Before the other three Brown Locusts could react, Angel and Trent unsheathed their blades and cut them down. Malice instructed the others to drag the bodies to the back and clean up the blood, which they did without hesitation.

"Sheep for the wolves," Angel stated.

Trent looked at her curiously, but surprised. "Damn. Sis, when did you become so philosophical?"

She shrugged her shoulders. "It comes and goes."

Trent and Malice laughed, but Angel maintained a straight face, a look they were used to seeing, so it hadn't alarming either of them.

"Well, I'm pretty sure ole Junior Master Nom Pi Chou's uncle will get the message when his nephew don't return," Malice said, while looking at the dead bodies being fed through the grinder, on the rear side were hog pens His thoughts were far from war or bloodshed. He was thinking about a future with the woman he loved . . . Angel.

The High Council was back in session. Headmaster Hia walked around the council table, stopping behind certain members' chairs. He could feel the uneasiness his presence caused them.

"The lack of not knowing one's intention brings uncertainty and fear. I forewarned all you of, we are all replaceable," Hia said. He stopped behind Vai Ki Hun's chair. "Master Vai Ki Hun, would you like to share with the council members the report you received from one of your informants?" asked Hia.

Although she didn't like being in the spotlight, Vai held her composure. "According to my source, General Chan Chou's nephew, Nom Chou, and his personal guards are dead," she stated clearly in Chinese.

Hia tapped the back of her chair before walking off. He sat down at the head of the council table. "Now you see what I forewarned all of you about. Don't take this feud between the Chou and Po Clan lightly. Learn the history before walking into a dragon's den. You all are dismissed," he said.

The council members stood and bowed towards the headmaster before leaving. Hia, himself, closed his eyes and enjoyed the silence. He knew which members could be trusted and which couldn't. "Now, what to do with them?" he questioned himself aloud.

General Chan Chou decided to take the day off from work. Although he had gone in his thoughts of victory over his enemies made him feel like celebrating. One of the Brown Locusts who were dressed in the tan ninja suit opened the car door for him in front of his home. He got out and bowed to the assassin.

Ninjas surrounded the three story mansion. All three balconies were lined with the tan ninja suit wearing assassins. On top of the mansion was the flag with a brown locust on the front and back.

"Honey, I'm home!" Chan yelled as he walked in the mansion.

Hearing her husband's voice, she jumped up out of bed. "He's home," she said in a hushed tone of voice. Her young lover jumped up and got dressed in a hurry. "I will see you again, luv. Soon," she promised. She kissed him passionately on the lips before letting him out through the balcony door. She ran and jumped in the shower.

General Chan walked up the stairs. When he entered the bedroom his wife was standing in the middle of the room toweling herself dry. He licked his lips, looking at her nude body. He closed the distance between them quickly, but when he tried to fulfill his desire, she backed out of his embrace. "I'm sorry, my husband, but I'm tired and I need to rest."

Mad and frustrated, Chan stormed out of the house and left.

CHAPTER FIFTEEN

Tabitha and Malice had made it back to their grandparents' house. Her first thought of the estate had been somewhat nice, but now that she was taking her time touring the place, it was livelier than she'd thought. There was artwork in several rooms and lining the hallways. It was amazing.

In every room they entered there were maids tending their chores and they received heartwarming smiles.

"Tabitha, I'm glad you're enjoying the tour of this old place," her grandmother said, as she turned around to face her. "It is nothing of a surprise to your bigheaded cousin. He used to run through these halls, making enough fuss to drive us all crazy."

Imagining Malice as a child running up and down the halls playing, Tabitha couldn't help but laugh. "Yes, this is a beautiful home, Grandma."

Her grandmother looked at the portrait of her husband and herself in their younger years. "The memories this old place has and the secrets hidden beneath these walls," she said staring in Tabitha's eyes.

"I bet," Tabitha replied, staring back into her grandmother's eyes.

The elderly woman turned around, breaking eye contact. "Well, let's move along. This place takes a lifetime to explore. Something I'm running short on," she said and started walking.

They came to a padlocked door, and her grandmother stopped in front of it and faced Tabitha again. "Tabitha, swear to me you will never speak a word of what lies behind this door. If you cannot swear, I cannot unlock it. Do I have your trust in keeping this secret, Tabitha Greene?"

Not wanting to seem overly excited or curious, Tabitha hesitated before she answered her grandmother. "I swear, Grandmother. You have my vow of secrecy."

"Very well then," she replied. She pulled out a single key and inserted it into the keyhole of the padlock. The padlock released and her grandmother removed it from the door. "You must open and walk through this door yourself, Tabitha."

Tabitha reached for the doorknob, but her grandmother grabbed her hand. "Know that once you walk through that door, there is no returning from what shall be revealed," she forewarned.

"Understood, Grandma," Tabitha replied and grabbed the doorknob. She turned the doorknob and gently pushed on the door. It screeched on its hinges as it opened inward. She stepped inside and flipped the light switch on.

The elderly woman heard her gasp for air. It wasn't five minutes later that Tabitha came out of the room with a look of pure wonderment sketched on her face. "What in the world?"

"Shh, my child. Untold secrets." Her grandmother cut her off while flipping the light switch off and closing the door. She placed the padlock back in place before turning to look Tabitha in the eyes again. In them, she saw the many questions. "Untold secrets that you must take to the grave, my child. Now, let's return to the menfolk. We can't leave them alone by themselves. They find all sorts of mischief to get into."

They took a different route than the way they had come. Tabitha noticed, but didn't bother questioning. From what she had just laid eyes on, there was no question she wanted answered more than those she had for what sat behind the padlocked door.

She and her grandmother met up with Kenneth and her grandfather in the den. They were sitting, having a glass of Paul Mason on ice, and talking about football. Something Tabitha wouldn't have never thought Kenneth found interest in.

"You see what I mean? Leave them alone for thirty minutes and this is what you get," her grandmother said. She walked over and stood in front of Kenneth. "And you, Kenneth Freeman, I hope you're planning on keeping him company for the rest of the day until he sobers up."

Kenneth's smile changed quickly. His grandmother cocked her head to the right with a smile on her face. "Like I thought." She and Tabitha sat with them.

Tabitha entertained them with telling them about her past. Most of which neither were happy to hear of because of all the drama and death it held. It was so sad, her grandmother grabbed two glasses of Sherrie; one for her, and the other for Tabitha.

They all sat and drank while listening to Tabitha reminisce. Feeling the tipsiness coming on, Kenneth reminded Tabitha they had business to tend to. So, they said their goodbyes and promised to come back to visit them soon.

"Tabitha don't let this knucklehead forget to bring you back soon," she said, standing on the front porch.

"I promise you, I won't, Grandma. You have a great evening," Tabitha replied, before getting in the car.

The Sherrie was definitely starting to kick in on her because she wasn't a drinker at all.

Kenneth hugged his grandmother and kissed her on the cheek. He also promised he wouldn't forget to come back soon. He hopped in behind the wheel and pulled off.

"What's on your mind, Tab?" asked Kenneth. He'd taken notice of her pondering demeanor when she and their grandmother had come into the den.

"Just thinking about my fly life. It's been a real pain in the ass ever since we met. Not to mention, the Sherrie is kicking my ass. I'll be the first to admit, I'm not drinker," Tabitha replied teasingly, but to a degree, she felt that way.

Kenneth laughed. "I kind of figured that much." Realizing she wasn't going to be much for talking, he turned on the music and let it take the place of the silence.

**

Ma Sune and her daughter, Yishi, sparred before the Sune Clan. Ma Sune's twin sister, Nia, and their mother, Mae Za Sune, sat amongst the clan members enjoying the entertainment. Mother and daughter were equally matched in the martial arts and weaponry. Neither was able to get a true strike on their opponent.

Ma Sune went for a front sweep, and Yishi jumped over and came down with a knee, attempting to strike her mother in the jaw. Quickly, Ma Sune rolled left to avoid the contact. As she stood back on her feet, Yishi came at her with a flurry of lightning fast kicks that she couldn't help but maneuver away from. Tired of evading, Ma Sune blocked a side kick and countered with an open palm strike, aiming for Yishi's knee. Yishi, being quick on her feet, turned a series of backward flips and landed, facing her mother, thirty feet away.

After Ma Sune and her daughter Yishi Pe Sune ended their sparring match, Ma Sune stepped aside, leaving Yishi standing on the platform by herself.

Without having to be asked or told what was expected of her, she began the performance. She started at a calm state, performing the Dance of the Mantis in its peaceful state. As the dance went on, she changed the tempo but maintained the fluent and fluid movement.

Everyone watched her perform, honoring the spirit of the Green Mantis. Yishi flowed like water and moved with the swiftness of the wind, and the emotion she put into it was like pure fire radiating from her spirit. Slowly, she began returning to the calm state of the dance. Once her breathing returned to normal, she prostrated, stood back to her feet, and bowed before joining her mother off to the side.

The two women sat comfortably on their knees, on the mats before them, as Mae Za Sune hobbled up on the platform and leaned forward on her cherry oak wood staff.

"There is always delight in watching the true art of The Mantis in action. It is the spirit within us all. However, we have a deeper spiritual side that comes from our kindred spirits, the Black Dragon. I pray to live to see the Green Mantis and Black Dragon Spirit reunite under the blood oath!" Mae Za Sune exclaimed before bowing.

Everyone remained sitting silently, knowing the elder wasn't done speaking. Mae Za Sune began to reminisce. She remembered the first day her daughter, Khia, one of her triplets, had come home with Hia at her side.

Han, without fear, had asked for the blessings of the Sune Clan to marry her daughter. His handsome dark features and seriousness was undeniable.

Besides, everyone knew Han Xi Po to be one of the greatest warriors the Po Clan had ever given birth to, so Khia would be safe. Not saying Khia couldn't defend for herself, because indeed, she was a force to be reckoned with. She and her triplet sisters, Ma and Nia, were great warriors of the Sune Clan.

Although knowing those things, Mae Za Sune had told Han he'd have to prove worthy of her daughter's flower. She could never forget the serious and confident look in the young man's eyes. Han had accepted the challenge. Together, they walked into the courtyard where the challenge had begun immediately after she had given the command. Han had fought with the true fierceness of the Black Dragon Spirit. He hadn't grabbed a weapon to defend himself against the weapons The Green Mantises wielded. He only used his spirit, soul, mind, and body. The young master was phenomenal...

Mae Za Sune had to fight back the tears and emotion. "My beloved daughter, Master Khia Li Sune Po and her husband, Master Han Xi Po, shall never be forgotten! Let us take this moment to honor an oath that shall remain unbroken because of their matrimony in spirit, soul, mind, body and death! The blood oath lives forever!" Mae Za Sune exclaimed raising her staff above her head.

The entire Sune Clan stood to their feet and began chanting, "Blood oath," over and over. Nobody knew what had really happened to Khia and Han, but they were determined to find out. Yishi began to think about her cousin, Saki. *It seems like forever since I've seen her,* she thought.

The thought of reuniting with her cousin fueled her ambition to make it come true. *And whoever tries to stand in the way, shall die by my sword,* Yishi swore silently before she thrust the blade of her sword in the air, and chanted, Blood oath!" louder than all.

To Be Continued…
Ruthless Hearts 2
Coming Soon

Excerpts from Ruthless Hearts 2: The Blood Oath

There's was a knock on the front door.

"Don't worry. I'll get it."

Jennifer ran to the door. As she opened the door, a ninja star missed her face by a hair and got stuck in the frame of the door.

Quickly, she slammed the door shut and locked it. She stood with her back against the wall in panic mode.

"Tabby, they're here!"

Tabitha locked Jennifer in the bathroom and told her not to come out until she knocked on the door and her voice was heard. She hurried to the walk-in closet and grabbed her sword. Barefooted, she exited the house through the backdoor. There was no one in sight.

Tabitha took a deep breath. She knew the only way she would draw the assassins out into the open was if she made herself an easy target. With that thought in mind, focused, she stepped off the back porch, into the open backyard. Not a second later, the ninja stars came flying towards her.

She evaded the oncoming silent instruments of death by diving out of its path. She rolled around on the grass, evading the steady flow of stars.

After the two assassins had thrown all of the ninja stars, they flipped off the roof of Jennifer's house and landed on their feet before her.

Tabitha unsheathed her sword. "Can we talk about this, guys?"

Their response to her question was to unsheathed their blades while circling about her.

"I guess not." Tabitha said as they attacked.

Coming Soon…

Submission Guideline

Submit the first three chapters of your completed manuscript to ldpsubmissions@gmail.com, subject line: Your book's title. The manuscript must be in a .doc file and sent as an attachment. Document should be in Times New Roman, double spaced and in size 12 font. Also, provide your synopsis and full contact information. If sending multiple submissions, they must each be in a separate email.

Have a story but no way to send it electronically? You can still submit to LDP/Ca$h Presents. Send in the first three chapters, written or typed, of your completed manuscript to:

LDP: Submissions Dept
Po Box 870494
Mesquite, Tx 75187

DO NOT send original manuscript. Must be a duplicate.

Provide your synopsis and a cover letter containing your full contact information.

Thanks for considering LDP and Ca$h Presents.

Ruthless Hearts

BOW DOWN TO MY GANGSTA

By **Ca$h**

TORN BETWEEN TWO

By **Coffee**

BLOOD STAINS OF A SHOTTA **III**

By **Jamaica**

STEADY MOBBIN **III**

By **Marcellus Allen**

RENEGADE BOYS IV

By Meesha

BLOOD OF A BOSS **VI**

SHADOWS OF THE GAME II

By **Askari**

LOYAL TO THE GAME **IV**

LIFE OF SIN **III**

By **T.J. & Jelissa**

A DOPEBOY'S PRAYER **II**

By **Eddie "Wolf" Lee**

IF LOVING YOU IS WRONG… **III**

By **Jelissa**

TRUE SAVAGE **VII**

By **Chris Green**

BLAST FOR ME **III**

DUFFLE BAG CARTEL **IV**

HEARTLESS GOON **II**

By **Ghost**

A HUSTLER'S DECEIT III

KILL ZONE **II**

BAE BELONGS TO ME III

SOUL OF A MONSTER III

By **Aryanna**

THE COST OF LOYALTY **III**

By **Kweli**

A GANGSTER'S SYN III

THE SAVAGE LIFE II

By **J-Blunt**

KING OF NEW YORK V

RISE TO POWER III

COKE KINGS IV

BORN HEARTLESS II

By **T.J. Edwards**

GORILLAZ IN THE BAY IV

De'Kari

THE STREETS ARE CALLING II

Duquie Wilson

KINGPIN KILLAZ IV

STREET KINGS III

PAID IN BLOOD III

CARTEL KILLAZ II

Hood Rich

SINS OF A HUSTLA II

ASAD

TRIGGADALE III

Elijah R. Freeman

KINGZ OF THE GAME IV

Playa Ray

SLAUGHTER GANG IV

RUTHLESS HEART II

By Willie Slaughter

THE HEART OF A SAVAGE II

By Jibril Williams

FUK SHYT II

By Blakk Diamond

THE DOPEMAN'S BODYGAURD II

By Tranay Adams

TRAP GOD II

By Troublesome

YAYO II

By S. Allen

GHOST MOB

Stilloan Robinson

KINGPIN DREAMS

By Paper Boi Rari

CREAM

By Yolanda Moore

<u>Available Now</u>

<u>RESTRAINING ORDER **I & II**</u>

By **CA$H & Coffee**

LOVE KNOWS NO BOUNDARIES **I II & III**

By **Coffee**

RAISED AS A GOON I, II, III & IV

BRED BY THE SLUMS I, II, III

BLAST FOR ME I & II

ROTTEN TO THE CORE I II III

A BRONX TALE I, II, III

DUFFEL BAG CARTEL I II III

HEARTLESS GOON

A SAVAGE DOPEBOY

HEARTLESS GOON

By **Ghost**

LAY IT DOWN **I & II**

LAST OF A DYING BREED

BLOOD STAINS OF A SHOTTA I & II

By **Jamaica**

LOYAL TO THE GAME

LOYAL TO THE GAME II

LOYAL TO THE GAME III

LIFE OF SIN I, II

By **TJ & Jelissa**

BLOODY COMMAS I & II

SKI MASK CARTEL I II & III

KING OF NEW YORK I II,III IV

RISE TO POWER I II

COKE KINGS I II III

BORN HEARTLESS

By **T.J. Edwards**

IF LOVING HIM IS WRONG…I & II

LOVE ME EVEN WHEN IT HURTS I II III

By **Jelissa**

WHEN THE STREETS CLAP BACK I & II III

By **Jibril Williams**

A DISTINGUISHED THUG STOLE MY HEART I II & III

LOVE SHOULDN'T HURT I II III IV

RENEGADE BOYS I II III

By **Meesha**

A GANGSTER'S CODE I &, II III

A GANGSTER'S SYN I II

THE SAVAGE LIFE

By **J-Blunt**

PUSH IT TO THE LIMIT

By **Bre' Hayes**

BLOOD OF A BOSS **I, II, III, IV, V**

SHADOWS OF THE GAME

By **Askari**

THE STREETS BLEED MURDER **I, II & III**

THE HEART OF A GANGSTA I II& III

By **Jerry Jackson**

CUM FOR ME

CUM FOR ME 2

CUM FOR ME 3

CUM FOR ME 4

CUM FOR ME 5

An **LDP Erotica Collaboration**

BRIDE OF A HUSTLA **I II & II**

THE FETTI GIRLS **I, II& III**

CORRUPTED BY A GANGSTA I, II III, IV

BLINDED BY HIS LOVE

By **Destiny Skai**

WHEN A GOOD GIRL GOES BAD

By **Adrienne**

THE COST OF LOYALTY I II

By Kweli

A GANGSTER'S REVENGE **I II III & IV**

THE BOSS MAN'S DAUGHTERS

THE BOSS MAN'S DAUGHTERS II

THE BOSSMAN'S DAUGHTERS III

THE BOSSMAN'S DAUGHTERS IV

THE BOSS MAN'S DAUGHTERS **V**

A SAVAGE LOVE **I & II**

BAE BELONGS TO ME I II

A HUSTLER'S DECEIT I, II, III

WHAT BAD BITCHES DO I, II, III

SOUL OF A MONSTER I II

KILL ZONE

By **Aryanna**

A KINGPIN'S AMBITON

A KINGPIN'S AMBITION **II**

I MURDER FOR THE DOUGH

By **Ambitious**

TRUE SAVAGE

TRUE SAVAGE II

TRUE SAVAGE **III**

TRUE SAVAGE **IV**

TRUE SAVAGE **V**

TRUE SAVAGE **VI**

By **Chris Green**

A DOPEBOY'S PRAYER

By **Eddie "Wolf" Lee**

THE KING CARTEL **I, II & III**

By **Frank Gresham**

THESE NIGGAS AIN'T LOYAL **I, II & III**

By **Nikki Tee**

GANGSTA SHYT **I II &III**

By **CATO**

THE ULTIMATE BETRAYAL

By **Phoenix**

BOSS'N UP **I , II & III**

By **Royal Nicole**

I LOVE YOU TO DEATH

By Destiny J

I RIDE FOR MY HITTA

I STILL RIDE FOR MY HITTA

By **Misty Holt**

LOVE & CHASIN' PAPER

By **Qay Crockett**

TO DIE IN VAIN

SINS OF A HUSTLA

By **ASAD**

BROOKLYN HUSTLAZ

By **Boogsy Morina**

BROOKLYN ON LOCK I & II

By **Sonovia**

GANGSTA CITY

By **Teddy Duke**

A DRUG KING AND HIS DIAMOND I & II III

A DOPEMAN'S RICHES

HER MAN, MINE'S TOO I, II

CASH MONEY HO'S

By Nicole Goosby

TRAPHOUSE KING **I II & III**

KINGPIN KILLAZ I II III

STREET KINGS I II

PAID IN BLOOD **I II**

CARTEL KILLAZ

By **Hood Rich**

LIPSTICK KILLAH **I, II, III**

CRIME OF PASSION I & II

By **Mimi**

STEADY MOBBN' **I, II, III**

By **Marcellus Allen**

WHO SHOT YA **I, II, III**

Renta

GORILLAZ IN THE BAY **I II III**

DE'KARI

TRIGGADALE I II

Elijah R. Freeman

GOD BLESS THE TRAPPERS I, II, III

THESE SCANDALOUS STREETS I, II, III

FEAR MY GANGSTA I, II, III

THESE STREETS DON'T LOVE NOBODY I, II

BURY ME A G I, II, III, IV, V

A GANGSTA'S EMPIRE I, II, III, IV

THE DOPEMAN'S BODYGAURD

Tranay Adams

THE STREETS ARE CALLING

Duquie Wilson

MARRIED TO A BOSS... I II III

By Destiny Skai & Chris Green

KINGZ OF THE GAME I II III

Playa Ray

SLAUGHTER GANG I II III

RUTHLESS HEART

By Willie Slaughter

THE HEART OF A SAVAGE

By Jibril Williams

FUK SHYT

By Blakk Diamond

DON'T F#CK WITH MY HEART I II

By Linnea

ADDICTED TO THE DRAMA I II III

By Jamila

YAYO

By S. Allen

TRAP GOD

By Troublesome

BOOKS BY LDP'S CEO, CA$H

TRUST IN NO MAN

TRUST IN NO MAN 2

TRUST IN NO MAN 3

BONDED BY BLOOD

SHORTY GOT A THUG

THUGS CRY

THUGS CRY 2

THUGS CRY 3

TRUST NO BITCH

TRUST NO BITCH 2

TRUST NO BITCH 3

TIL MY CASKET DROPS

RESTRAINING ORDER

RESTRAINING ORDER 2

IN LOVE WITH A CONVICT

Coming Soon

BONDED BY BLOOD 2

BOW DOWN TO MY GANGSTA